THE DEATH OF HOPE

Before there was the Phantom Menace, there was . . .

STAR WARS®

JEDI APPRENTICE

. . . and more to come

JEDI APPRENTICE SPECIAL EDITION
#1 Deceptions

JEDI APPRENTICE

The Death of Hope

Jude Watson

SCHOLASTIC INC.

New York Toronto London Auckland Sydney
Mexico City New Delhi Hong Kong Buenos Aires

ISBN 0-439-13934-1

Cover art by Cliff Nielsen.

12 11 10 9 8 7 6 5 4 3 2 1   1 2 3 4 5 6/0

Printed in the U.S.A.
First Scholastic printing, October 2001

THE DEATH OF HOPE

Obi-Wan Kenobi kept his eyes on his Master, Qui-Gon Jinn. He did not like to break Qui-Gon's concentration, but he was impatient to know what his Master was thinking.

They sat in the small, elegant waiting room at the Supreme Governor's residence on the planet of New Apsolon. A lightsaber lay on a small table next to Qui-Gon. Qui-Gon didn't move his eyes from it. Every few minutes he would pick up the hilt and hold it in his hand. He had even activated it a few times, losing himself in the sapphire glow. Then he would deactivate it and, still holding it tightly, get up to pace the room. In just moments he would abruptly whirl, slam the lightsaber down on the table again, and sit.

The process had been going on for some time now.

Obi-Wan was sure that his Master was formulating a plan. Jedi Knight Tahl had been kidnapped. They knew who the culprit was — Balog, the Chief Security Controller of New Apsolon. They just did not know why, or where Balog had taken her. Tahl had not been able to leave any clues behind.

Obi-Wan was trying to come up with the best course of action himself. He hadn't gotten far. They both doubted that Balog was acting alone, but they didn't know who he was in league with. Confidently, Obi-Wan waited for Qui-Gon to conclude his internal strategy session. He had seen it in the past. His Master would turn and look at him directly. His gaze would be sharp and focused. He would crisply outline the best way to proceed.

Qui-Gon turned to him at last. "I should have gone with her to that meeting," he said sadly.

Startled, Obi-Wan could only shake his head. Qui-Gon never wasted time on what they *should* have done. "But Balog told us that only one Jedi was allowed."

"I should have made her leave the planet when it was clear her identity was compromised." Tahl had gone undercover and pretended to be one of the Absolutes. They had once been the secret police of New Apsolon, and had since been outlawed. They had never disbanded, though, and had continued to meet in secret, gathering power over the years.

"But she would not have left." Obi-Wan spoke patiently. He wasn't telling Qui-Gon anything his Master did not know already. "We need to contact the Temple. They will send help."

"Not yet." Qui-Gon's tone was firm. "We know now that there are many here who hate and resent the Jedi. If more Jedi arrive, it will make it harder for us to find contacts to help us. Especially among the Workers."

"But a Jedi Knight is missing," Obi-Wan said. "It is our duty to contact the Council."

"And we will," Qui-Gon told him. "But we need twenty-four hours first. We will find her, Obi-Wan. I can *feel* her. I know she is alive. I know she will find a way to help us once we get on her trail." Qui-Gon returned to his pacing. "We should talk to Balog's assistant again."

"We've already spoken to him twice," Obi-Wan said quietly. "Both of us felt sure he had nothing more to tell us." It would feel strange and awkward to tell his own Master to focus, as Qui-Gon had told him so many times. Yet Obi-Wan felt that Qui-Gon needed to slow down. His Master's thoughts were circling in a pattern that would lead nowhere. Obi-Wan could see it clearly, for he had been taught by Qui-Gon how to think calmly in the midst of panic, how to find a way out.

Qui-Gon knew this. Why couldn't he practice it?

Obi-Wan could see anguish and desperation on Qui-Gon's face, and something it took a beat for him to recognize — indecision. With a sense of shock, he realized that Qui-Gon did not know what to do next. Qui-Gon always knew what to do next.

Obi-Wan decided to use a method Qui-Gon had for helping to focus. *If you don't know which way to turn, review what you know.*

"This is what we know," Obi-Wan began, even though he could tell that Qui-Gon was only half-listening. Obi-Wan was starting to worry about his Master, and that was taking his own attention from the task at hand. "There are two factions battling for power on New Apsolon — the Workers and the Civilized. The government is in disarray. Before we arrived on New Apsolon, the Supreme Governor, Ewane, was assassinated. He was a Worker who had been imprisoned for many years by the Absolutes. After his death, his close ally, Roan, was elected. Though Roan was a Civilized, he had fought for the Workers to become full citizens of New Apsolon. He took in Ewane's twin daughters, Alani and Eritha. But Alani and Eritha still feared for their lives. They contacted the Jedi to escort them off-planet."

Qui-Gon stirred impatiently. "We know all this, Obi-Wan."

Obi-Wan had once been impatient when Qui-Gon repeated facts to him. But Qui-Gon had always ignored his impatience and continued. Now it was Obi-Wan's turn to push forward.

"Tahl came to the planet alone and infiltrated the disbanded Absolutes, who had gone underground. After we arrived, Eritha and Alani were kidnapped. Roan disappeared to pay the ransom and was killed. Shortly afterward, the twins were released, which led us to believe that Roan was the true target all along. Tahl's identity as a Jedi was discovered but she escaped. She went to a peace negotiation meeting of Workers and Civilized organized by Balog. Only we have discovered that there was no meeting. Balog lied in order to kidnap Tahl. The question is, why? Balog was a Worker. It doesn't seem likely he'd kidnap a Jedi."

"Anything is likely on this planet," Qui-Gon said grimly, shoving Tahl's lightsaber into his belt.

"Another question is whether Tahl's kidnapping is linked to the twins," Obi-Wan went on. "Was Balog responsible for that, too? If so, he is most likely responsible for the murder of Roan.

Irini gave us information from the Workers that suggested that the person who masterminded the twins' kidnapping was in the inner circle here. But why Balog?"

Qui-Gon's gaze was clear now. "We don't know the answers to any of these questions," he said. "But it seems clear that it is all linked — Ewane's assassination, Roan's murder, the kidnapping of the twins — and that someone or some organization is behind these things. They want power."

"So kidnapping Tahl is a way for them to get that power? How?"

"Uncovering the answers will take longer than a day. Time we don't have. We need to find Tahl first." Qui-Gon turned back to Obi-Wan. "What was the principal method the Absolutes used to keep the Workers in line?"

"Probe droids," Obi-Wan answered after a moment. "The droids on New Apsolon are technologically advanced. They can track subjects and attack to stun or kill. The vital information of all Workers was kept in files, and with that information a probe droid could be programmed to target a specific person —" Obi-Wan slowly rose. "Of course. Balog is a Worker. If we can get his vitals —"

"And a probe droid," Qui-Gon finished.

A soft voice came from behind them. "But they are illegal now."

It was Alani. The slight sixteen-year-old stood in the doorway for a moment, dressed in a simple tunic, her golden hair braided and coiled around her head. She had dark smudges under her eyes. The twins had stayed awake mourning Roan, and the news of Tahl's disappearance had devastated them. Tahl and the twins had a special bond.

She took a few steps into the room. "I didn't mean to overhear. I came to see if I can bring you refreshment."

"We'd rather have a probe droid," Qui-Gon said.

"I might be able to help you with that as well," Alani said. "At least, I know someone who can find one. Lenz."

"Lenz," Obi-Wan said, repeating the name. Lenz had been among the Workers in a secret meeting he and Qui-Gon had overheard.

"He is the leader of the Workers," Alani said. "He will say he doesn't know how to get one, but that's a lie. Tell him I sent you."

"You know him well?" Qui-Gon asked.

"Lenz took us in when our father was imprisoned," Alani said. "So yes, I know him well. We are not in touch anymore, but he will help you if

I ask him to. The trouble will be finding him. He moves from place to place."

"We have no time to waste," Obi-Wan said in frustration. Would they need a probe droid to track Lenz, too?

Alani frowned, thinking. "Irini will know how to find him. She will be at her job at the Absolute Museum by now."

The Jedi knew Irini. But knowing her didn't mean she would help them. She was a prominent leader in the Worker movement, and she had made it clear that she did not consider the Jedi her allies. They suspected her of trying to kill them when they had first arrived on New Apsolon. But there was no one else to turn to.

CHAPTER 2

It had been a time of great confusion for Qui-Gon. It had been as though his body temperature had risen, as if there was a fever in his blood. He had been restless and irritable. Deep meditation was hard to sustain. Tired of waiting for a mission to distract him, he had taken Obi-Wan on a survival trip to Ragoon-6, hoping the discipline would calm his mind and body. It had not.

The first vision appeared on Ragoon-6. He saw Tahl in distress. In his vision, he caught and held her. Her body felt so weak. He was filled with helplessness and fear.

When he returned to the Temple, anxious to find her, he discovered that Tahl was on the verge of leaving on a mission to New Apsolon. Qui-Gon could not interfere. Yet after she had gone he was once again visited by that same disturbing vision. He knew she was headed for danger. He knew that she would need him. He knew she would resist his help.

He did not need Yoda to tell him that visions should not serve as a guide for behavior. He did not listen to the Council when they cautioned him to wait. He left for New Apsolon, drawn by a compulsion he did not understand. He had to follow her.

But the most important thing had not become clear. Why had the visions of Tahl in trouble come to him, haunted him, driven him? Why did just the sight of her suddenly irritate him and warm him at the same time?

Then, in one blinding moment, he had received his answer. He had felt a shock so deep it seemed his body could not contain it. He had found that he was not just a Jedi, but a man. And the fever in his blood was Tahl.

Courage was something a Jedi did not think about. It was simply the will to do right. It was the discipline to move forward. Qui-Gon had never had to reach for it; it had always been there, ready for him. It deserted him when he asked to speak to Tahl alone.

He had poured out his heart as only a quiet man could. He had used few words. The time it took for her to respond had *seemed endless. Then she had taken a step forward, taken his hand, and pledged her life to his. They would have one life, together, she had said.*

What an astonishing lesson, Qui-Gon thought, to find that joy was such a simple thing. It sprang from a single, shining source. She said yes. She said yes.

As they walked the short distance to the museum, Qui-Gon had to discipline himself severely to recall his Jedi training. He knew that his Padawan was troubled by his behavior. It was true that for the first time since he was a young Temple student, he was having trouble with his focus.

In the midst of every battle, every trouble, Qui-Gon had always been able to find his calm center. When he reached for it now, it was gone. Replacing it was a core of turbulent, angry chaos, fueled by his guilt and his fear.

This was the time he must operate at the peak of his efficiency. This was the time that called for his most intense focus.

The cold fear that lay deep within him was not just for Tahl. He was also afraid of his own doubt.

He had never been so at a loss because he had never felt like this before. Only hours ago, he and Tahl had pledged their lives to each other. The emotion and the need had surprised them both. Once they had accepted it, it had felt like the most natural thing in the world. Qui-Gon was astonished to discover that he had found one person who mattered to him more than anything else in the galaxy.

And now he had lost her.

"Qui-Gon?"

Obi-Wan jolted him out of his jumbled thoughts. He saw that he had paused in front of the museum's wide double doors.

"The museum is closed," Obi-Wan said. "It's too early."

"It opens in fifteen minutes. No doubt the guides are here."

The museum had been built shortly after the government of Apsolon reorganized and became New Apsolon. As a show of good faith, the government opened the doors of the hated headquarters of the Absolutes. People were free to come and acknowledge the horrors that had been done there. It was, the leaders felt, a way to prevent the horrors from happening again. Former victims of Absolute repression had come forward and obtained jobs as guides to the complex. This was how the Jedi had met Irini.

Qui-Gon pressed the off-hours signal button. He heard it ring inside. No one came.

Qui-Gon pounded on the door. He could not wait fifteen minutes. He could not wait one second more than he had to.

The door slid open. Irini stood in her guide uniform. She glowered at the Jedi.

"The museum is not open yet."

"We saw that," Qui-Gon said, striding past her.

"This is outrageous," Irini said. "I came to you with information about Roan's murder. I trusted you. The next thing I knew, you ran off and security threw me out of the Governor's house."

"Balog has kidnapped Tahl," Qui-Gon told her, his voice struggling to remain even.

Irini gasped. Then, after a visible struggle, her face resumed its smooth mask. Her voice hardened. "I see," she said after a moment. "So Balog is the traitor to our cause. He is the one behind the kidnapping of the twins and Roan's murder."

Despite Irini's control, Qui-Gon sensed that this news had deeply upset her.

"He will be a formidable enemy," she murmured.

"The only thing we know for sure is that Balog kidnapped Tahl," Obi-Wan said. "We don't know why."

"We need a probe droid," Qui-Gon said. "It's

the fastest way to track Balog. Alani told us Lenz could get one."

"Lenz does not keep me informed as to his movements," Irini said brusquely. "I am not his keeper."

Qui-Gon felt his impatience tighten another notch. Every minute that ticked by took Tahl farther from him, made her trail colder. Irini stood in the way.

He studied her for a moment. Irini's navy tunic was buttoned up to her neck, and her black hair was slicked back severely. There was not a flicker of warmth in her eyes. She was dedicated to the Workers' cause, and thought the Jedi were too friendly to the Civilized faction. Qui-Gon knew from experience how tough Irini could be. But he would not go away until he got what he wanted.

She saw something in his gaze and quickly turned away. "I have to work," she said.

"No." Qui-Gon's voice was soft, but it stopped her in her tracks. He told himself to go slowly. Irini would not respond to threats or intimidation. She would dig in her heels.

"Just hours ago you came to us with information," he said. "You trusted us. We trusted your information."

"Your Jedi has been kidnapped," Irini said, her head still turned away and her voice muffled. "I am sorry for that, but I am not responsible. It is Jedi business. One thing I do know — the Absolutes do not take kindly to betrayal."

"How did you know that Tahl infiltrated the Absolutes?" Qui-Gon asked urgently. He took three steps toward her in order to see her face. "And why do you think they had something to do with her kidnapping?"

She lifted her chin defiantly. "What does it matter? We are not on the same side, Jedi."

"But we are," Obi-Wan said. "You are against the Absolutes. If they kidnapped Tahl, she may know things that you want to know."

There was logic in what Obi-Wan said but Qui-Gon didn't think Irini would care. Yet something in Obi-Wan's words caused her to stop and give them a hard stare.

"I might be able to find Lenz," she said reluctantly.

"Then let's go," Qui-Gon said firmly. He had to keep pushing forward. He had to drown out his worst fears with action.

They had only caught a glimpse of Lenz the first time they'd seen him, but Qui-Gon remembered him well. His was not a face to forget. It had been marked by suffering and illness, but there was nobility and strength in it. His body was weak, yet his spirit had great power. In a crowd he might be ignored, but Qui-Gon knew from the first glance that he was a leader.

Lenz stood as Irini led the Jedi into a small room in the Worker section of the city. She had alerted him by comlink that they were coming, and why.

Lenz gave Irini a questioning look. "Now you trust the Jedi? What happened?"

"They have a good point," Irini said. "They have the best chance of finding Tahl. If Balog betrayed us for the Absolutes, we need to know."

Lenz kept his gaze on Irini. Slowly, he nodded. "Maybe."

His nerves on alert, Qui-Gon sensed something had passed between Irini and Lenz. It had been a wordless exchange of information. They knew each other very well, he realized. Well enough to speak without words, as he and his Padawan could.

"Irini tells me you want a probe droid," Lenz said.

Obi-Wan nodded. "Alani asked that you help us."

Lenz smiled slightly. "When both Irini and Alani ask me to do something, I have no choice but to obey." He gestured at them to sit at a battered metal table. "I must warn you, we run some danger of being arrested. Since Roan's murder the government has been cracking down on those who run the black market. Power is slipping out of their hands, and they think a show of it will save them. The United Legislature is locked in a battle to appoint Roan's successor."

"Many Workers think the time to strike is now," Irini said. "There are those who want us to conduct another campaign of industrial sabotage to get what we want. Of course we want a Worker to be appointed as Supreme Governor, but Lenz and I are urging caution. We will lose our support among the Civilized with another sabotage campaign. It worked once, but we do not feel it will work again. We don't want civil unrest."

"Yet we are very close to it," Lenz said.

"Do you think Balog is an Absolute?" Obi-Wan asked.

Lenz and Irini exchanged glances. "He was born a Worker," Irini said hesitantly. "And he was close to Ewane, the great Worker leader . . ."

"But yes, we think his allegiance has now changed," Lenz said grimly. "Once you told us that he had kidnapped Tahl, it all clicked into place. He has most likely been working for the Absolutes for some time. That's why he kidnapped Alani and Eritha. He had always planned to let them go — his real target was Roan."

"So he lured Roan to him through the ransom," Obi-Wan said. "Then he murdered him."

Qui-Gon remembered Balog's show of grief when they had found Roan's body. Balog was a good actor. But he'd have to be, if he'd been working with the secret organization of Absolutes all along.

"One thing puzzles me," Qui-Gon said. "Balog may be head of security, but he's no match for Tahl. Even without her lightsaber. How could he have overpowered her?"

"The Absolutes often used a paralyzing drug," Irini said. "You remain conscious but immobilized. It is easy to administer. If she turned her back on him for a moment . . ."

"Is the drug dangerous?" Qui-Gon asked the question, though he dreaded the answer.

"Not with one dose," Lenz said. "Or even two. The trouble is that it wears off, and if it is reused many times — especially over a short period of time — it can result in permanent damage. Muscle deterioration is one side effect." Lenz pointed down at himself. "As you can see."

"Lenz was one of the lucky ones," Irini added quietly. "There can be permanent damage to internal organs. They completely waste away in a short period of time. There were many who . . ." Her voice trailed off, and she flushed.

She is telling me that Tahl could die. Underneath the table, Qui-Gon gripped his hands together. Thinking of Tahl helpless, her mind active but her body deteriorating, made him want to rip the room apart.

The vision that had beckoned him to New Apsolon came back to him now. Tahl weak, her leg muscles unable to support her. She leaned against him, her hand curling around his neck. *It is too late for me, dear friend. . . .*

"You are hiding something from us," Qui-Gon said, gazing directly at Irini, then at Lenz. "What is it?"

"Nothing," Irini answered. "We have agreed to help you find a probe droid —"

"Yet there is something about the kidnapping that you know and we do not," Qui-Gon said, the anger escalating in his voice. "You admit that we stand the best chance of finding Tahl. Give us all the information we need, and the chances are greater still." He leaned forward. The time had come for a little intimidation. He did not like to use it, but his impatience had run its course. He needed to act, and these people could not stand in his way. "I remind you that it is never a good idea to cross the Jedi."

Obi-Wan picked up on his urgency. "We have lost one of our own," he said. "This is a serious matter to us."

The double threat from the two Jedi seemed to rock Lenz. He swallowed. "It is not something we know. It is something we suspect."

"Lenz —"

"No, Irini. They are right. They should know." Lenz silenced her with a look, then turned his attention back to the Jedi. "We know that the Absolutes used secret informers when they were in power. There is a list of those who informed. This list is encrypted so that it cannot be copied. Only a few in the government knew of this list, even fewer have seen it, and we think most of them — maybe all of them — are dead. One of them was Roan. Roan had it, but it was stolen before he died. We know that much."

"At first we thought Balog had been able to get it from Roan," Irini said. "Now we don't think so. Someone else did."

"We think Balog is looking for it," Lenz said. "After all, his name is on it. If that was discovered, he would lose all credibility among the Workers. Our word against Balog will not be enough to turn people against him. We need proof. He needs to destroy that proof. We think his ambitions lie higher than the office of Chief Security Controller. Whoever has the list has great power. It will be his or her choice to expose the informers or keep them secret, to bribe them for silence or look like a hero for exposing them. Careers and reputations will be destroyed. The list is said to contain some prominent names."

"What does Tahl have to do with this?" Obi-Wan asked.

"The list was in Absolute hands for a short time, then disappeared," Irini said. "We know this for sure. What if Balog thinks that Tahl has the list? It's the only explanation as to why Balog would capture her and yet keep her alive."

Qui-Gon shook his head. "If Tahl had the list, we would have known it."

"So you don't think she has it?" Lenz asked.

"Perhaps she doesn't *know* she has it," Irini guessed. "Perhaps she knows where it can be found. She just doesn't know the significance of it."

This news was disturbing. It meant that Balog could be keeping her alive only until he knew the truth. Tahl did not have that list. When he discovered that, he would kill her.

Qui-Gon saw by Obi-Wan's pale face that his Padawan had come to the same conclusion. He stood. "If your theory is right, Balog won't have much patience. Neither do I. Let's get that probe droid."

CHAPTER 3

Lenz and Irini led them deep into the Worker sector, near the outskirts of the city. The area had been abandoned by the Workers when better housing became available after the election of Ewane. Block after block of abandoned housing showed the effects of neglect and disorder. Half-demolished buildings stood next to intact ones whose windows were shattered or blown out completely. Rubble lay in the street, and stacks of durasteel sheeting were piled up in vacant lots.

"The government is planning to tear these down," Lenz said, gesturing at the devastated buildings. "The lawmakers can't agree on what to build instead, so the project is left half finished. But it has become a good place to hide for those who don't want to be found. Security sweeps are made frequently, so we must all be alert."

"How will we program the droid to find Balog?" Qui-Gon asked. "We don't have complete information on him. We know that vitals on Workers are stored somewhere. Who has access to them?"

"Everything you need you will be able to buy here," Lenz said.

He stopped in front of a partially demolished building and took a laser signal from his tunic. He activated the laser point and blinked it several times in a pattern against the stone front of the building. A concealed sensor in the wall caught the signal and, after a moment, blinked twice.

"We can enter," Lenz said.

Obi-Wan glanced at his Master. He was relieved to see that Qui-Gon seemed himself again. Most likely it was because they had taken action. He could sense the frustration inside Qui-Gon — as well as something else there, some desperation that Obi-Wan didn't understand. At least Qui-Gon was back in control. He had found the calm he needed to proceed. Later, when Tahl was safe, Obi-Wan would ask his Master why he'd had such trouble focusing. Qui-Gon would not mind the question. He knew that Obi-Wan would only ask in order to learn.

Lenz pushed open the door to the building. Obi-Wan noted that although the building appeared to be a ruin, the door was armored. The arming devices must have been released when the sensor blinked back an okay.

A staircase led upward, but Lenz turned to the side and accessed a doorway flush to the wall. A ramp led down to a lower level.

Lenz and Irini went first, and the Jedi followed. The ramp was lit with one dim glow rod attached to the wall. Obi-Wan strode down the sloping ramp, ready for anything.

A figure stepped out of the dimness. "Lenz. We haven't seen you here in a while."

"Greetings, Mota. You know I have forbidden the Workers to use illegal means to achieve our ends," Lenz said. "But my friends here need your help."

The man stepped closer. He was dressed in the unisuit that Obi-Wan had seen many Workers wear. His gray hair was tied behind him, and his body looked strong. There were two blasters tucked into his utility belt.

"You must be Jedi," he said, though Obi-Wan and Qui-Gon were dressed in the garments of space travelers. "Never thought I'd see the day the Jedi would need my help."

"We are grateful for anything you can provide us with," Qui-Gon said.

"Don't get me wrong. It will cost you. I'm in the business for one reason only. Credits. I'm the one who takes the risks. You can hitch rides around the galaxy, but my products aren't free."

"We are prepared to pay," Qui-Gon replied impatiently. "The speed of the transaction is more important than price."

"Then let's get to it."

Mota led the way down a long hallway into a large open space. Long metal tables stretched from one end of the space to the other. Isolated pieces of merchandise were laid out on the tables. There were some communication devices, some weaponry, and some pieces of tech equipment.

"As you can see, our stocks are low," Mota said.

Lenz looked at him sharply. "I'll say. Who is buying your weapons?"

Mota's return gaze was neutral. "Whoever has the credits. I don't ask questions."

"We need probe droids," Qui-Gon said.

"I only have one. Probe droids are hard to get." Mota strode to a table and picked up a droid. "It's in good shape, though. All ready for programming."

"They need the vitals of a citizen," Irini said. "Balog."

"The Chief Security Controller?" At last an emotion flickered over Mota's face: surprise.

But it smoothed out and became neutral again. "I have his stats. I can program the droid. The vitals will cost you more credits."

"They'll need swoops or landspeeders," Lenz said.

"Down below."

"Let's program the droid first," Qui-Gon said.

"Sure. Just let me see the credits." Mota named a figure, and Qui-Gon counted out the currency.

Mota pocketed the credits without counting them and turned to a data screen. He began to access files.

"The vitals on every citizen were entered into the main files of the Absolutes in the old days," Irini told them in a low voice. "It is illegal to access those files now, but that doesn't stop Mota. Having exact information on Balog will help greatly in tracking."

Mota downloaded the information in the data-pad into the droid, then programmed it. The probe droid beeped and revolved.

"When would you like to release the droid?" Mota asked.

"Immediately," Qui-Gon answered tersely.

Mota accessed a shuttered window, and the probe droid flew out. Mota handed the transmitter to Qui-Gon.

"Keep this on at all times, and the probe droid

will find you. If the droid is destroyed, it will tell you that, too. I've programmed the droid to make a preliminary search. If it can't pinpoint Balog in the city, it will be able to pinpoint his point of departure."

Qui-Gon nodded and hooked the transmitter onto his utility belt. "Now let's see about those speeders."

They followed another ramp down to a lower level. It was an identically sized space, this one filled with surface transport vehicles — swoops, landspeeders, gravsleds.

"Our inventory is pretty full, so you can take your pick," Mota said.

Qui-Gon quickly chose a landspeeder and a swoop. "We might need the agility for at least one of us," he told Obi-Wan. "The other will have room for Tahl." He turned to Mota. "These are guaranteed?"

"They're a few years old, but they won't let you down," Mota said. "My merchandise is the best."

"Glad to hear it," Qui-Gon said. "But we'll test them first."

Mota accessed double durasteel doors at the end of the space. "Go through that door to the backyard. You can test them there. Just watch out for security patrols overhead."

Obi-Wan slung his leg over the swoop and

adjusted the seat so that he had easy access to the controls in the handlebars. He revved up the repulsorlift engine as Qui-Gon started his landspeeder. He followed Qui-Gon as he zoomed out the double doors. They passed into a short tunnel and then burst into the open air. They found themselves in an open yard with high security fencing surrounding it.

Obi-Wan had ridden a swoop before and was used to the extra maneuverability. He pushed the swoop, making sharp turns and accelerating rapidly. He was glad to see that the vehicle handled well. Qui-Gon also seemed satisfied, and the two of them landed the transports and turned off the engines just as Irini and Lenz appeared in the yard.

"If you find the list with Tahl, what will you do with it?" Irini asked them anxiously.

"The list is not our first concern," Qui-Gon said.

"You must realize how much power resides in that list," Lenz said. "It cannot fall into the wrong hands."

"Do you promise to come to us first if you have it?" Irini asked.

"I cannot make that promise," Qui-Gon said. "But I will promise that we will keep it safe. The Jedi will volunteer to hold the list as a neutral party until the government appoints a successor to Roan."

Irini nodded reluctantly.

Obi-Wan caught sight of a blur in the sky. "I think the probe droid is returning already."

Qui-Gon looked up, his expression tense with expectation. The probe droid settled on the ground in front of him. He quickly bent to examine the readout.

"Balog has left the city," Qui-Gon said. "He's struck out over open country."

"That's strange," Lenz said. "Why would he leave his base of support?"

"Maybe he knows the Jedi are on his trail," Irini said.

Qui-Gon programmed the droid to continue tracking and sent it off again. Then he programmed the coordinates of Balog's last stop into his shipboard computer. He gave Obi-Wan the coordinates, and Obi-Wan did the same on his swoop.

Mota emerged from a door concealed in the wall of the building.

"How do you like the transports?" he asked.

"They're fine. We have a deal," Qui-Gon said, counting out the additional credits.

Mota placed the credits inside a pocket of his unisuit. Suddenly, the sensors on the wall began to glow. Mota watched as they beeped out a private code.

"Patrols in the vicinity," Mota said. "I suggest you leave." Without another word, he swiftly made his way back to the hidden door and disappeared.

"Don't worry, Mota, we'll be fine," Lenz muttered. "Irini, we'd better get out of here." He nodded at the Jedi. "You should take off. If the security patrol sees you with black market transports, you'll be detained, possibly even arrested."

"Thank you for your help," Obi-Wan said hastily as he mounted his swoop.

"Will you be all right?" Qui-Gon asked.

"We know this area well," Lenz assured them. "There is an exit through that fence that will bring us safely home. If I were you I'd go out the back way and stick to the alleys."

From a distance, they heard the sound of speeder engines.

"We'll be in touch," Qui-Gon told them.

The two transports lifted into the air. Qui-Gon led the way out. The narrow alley snaked out from the backyard of Mota's building, twisting and turning past the back sides of the crumbling buildings. They could hear security landspeeder engines nearby, but could not see them.

Finally, they emerged on a deserted street. Qui-Gon headed east toward the outskirts of the city. He pushed his engine to maximum and Obi-Wan followed.

With the security patrol well behind them, they reached the edge of the city and took off over open country. Obi-Wan felt his spirits rise as the wind blew in his face. He couldn't help but feel that Tahl was within their reach.

CHAPTER 4

By the time they reached the coordinates that the probe droid had given them, the droid had not returned with Balog's next position.

Qui-Gon halted his speeder, which hovered over the ground. Obi-Wan pulled up next to him. They were well outside the city in an unpopulated area. It was flat and dry, with only a few trees clumped here and there. In the far distance, they could see hills.

"We could wait here for the droid," Qui-Gon said to Obi-Wan. "Or we could track ourselves. If we're wrong, we'd have to double back. It could waste time."

Obi-Wan nodded. "Then we can't be wrong."

By the look on his Master's face, Obi-Wan knew it was the answer he'd wanted to hear.

Leaving the engines idling, the two Jedi jumped from their transports and examined the ground. Obi-Wan had been taught tracking at the Temple, but he'd also recently been on a tracking exercise with Qui-Gon on Ragoon-6. He was glad he'd had a chance to brush up on his skills.

"The probe droid has told us that Balog is traveling in an armored hoverscout," Qui-Gon said. "We know he was last heading roughly east. If we can find some evidence of scorch marks from the engine, we can track him. A vehicle of that weight takes a bigger power drive. There's a predictable pattern of acceleration and release of excess exhaust."

Obi-Wan examined the ground as he'd been taught, dividing it into sections and noticing each pebble, each disturbance of sand. He crouched down to examine a rock.

"Here," he said. He moved a step on. "And here."

Qui-Gon leaned over to examine the trail. "Yes. See how deeply the rocks have been marked. He accelerated here. Let's go."

They jumped back onto their transports and took off. Every so often they stopped to examine the surrounding ground. True to the pattern, they found evidence of exhaust on the rocks and ground. They knew they were still on Balog's trail.

The suns began to slip down into the sky. Obi-Wan scanned the horizon ahead. He saw a black shape heading their way. He didn't say anything for a moment. He hoped it was the droid but wasn't certain.

Qui-Gon's gaze was slightly sharper. "Here it comes," he called, relief in his voice. He halted the speeder and Obi-Wan pulled up beside him. In just minutes, the droid returned.

Qui-Gon consulted the readout. "He's stopped. Good. We might be able to catch up to him by dawn."

Qui-Gon released the probe droid again, then zoomed off to the next destination. Obi-Wan pushed his engine to follow. Balog was within their grasp.

They rode all night. It was Obi-Wan's second night without sleep. The three moons rose high in the purple sky, and the calls of night creatures came to him faintly. When weariness overcame him, he reached out to the Force to help him maintain a meditative state. He was alert enough to drive, yet was able to allow his body to rest even as he sped over the rocky ground. Qui-Gon did not appear tired in the least.

Dawn broke quickly on this world. The horizon turned red-orange, and the blazing color spread into the dark purple of the sky as the suns rose higher. The flat landscape had changed to foothills that grew larger and steeper as they rode. Trees were thick, and the Jedi had to use caution to keep up their speed.

"We are close, Padawan. Let's slow down a bit. Balog could be breaking camp." Qui-Gon slowed his engine, and Obi-Wan followed suit.

"We should go on foot from here. He should be over that next hill."

Obi-Wan jumped off his swoop gratefully. His legs felt stiff. The air was cold, and he moved quickly to warm his muscles.

They climbed the hill silently. Their footing had to be assured, for if they slipped, they could cause a small rock slide that would alert Balog of their presence.

They neared the top of the hill and Qui-Gon dropped to his hands and knees. Obi-Wan did the same. He slithered up to the top and peered over.

All he saw was an empty plain. There was no sign of Balog, even in the distance. He must have left long ago.

Qui-Gon dropped his head into his hands. He did not speak for a moment. Obi-Wan was disappointed, but he could see that his Master was distraught.

Obi-Wan was tired and hungry and cold. There was nothing he would like better right now than to set up the condenser unit for warmth, eat some rations, and settle on the ground for a good sleep of at least a few hours.

Instead, he put his hand on Qui-Gon's shoulder. He spoke softly. "Let's keep going."

"Yes," Qui-Gon said, his expression fierce. "Let's move on."

CHAPTER 5

Before the morning had passed, the probe droid returned with new coordinates. Balog was traveling quickly, with barely any stops. Obi-Wan could see Qui-Gon's frustration harden into cold resolve. He would not rest until they caught up with Balog. He would drive his body to the limit.

The temperature rose, and the combined power of the blazing suns bore down on Obi-Wan. He took a swallow of water from his rations. He felt light-headed from the heat and lack of sleep.

"Do you think Balog doesn't stop because he knows we're behind him?" he asked Qui-Gon.

"Or he has a destination in mind and knows he will be safe there," Qui-Gon responded. "It would be best for us to catch up to him before he reaches it."

Obi-Wan wanted to ask Qui-Gon more questions, but he stilled his curiosity. He sensed that talk would disrupt his Master's concentration. They were using the probe droid, but they also needed their own tracking skills to keep moving. Time and time again they needed to exit their transports and make their way over the ground. Obi-Wan now realized how different a training exercise was from reality. He had to make absolutely sure that he didn't miss a thing, and that what he did read from the ground was correct. Tahl's life depended on it.

As the first sun began to set, the probe droid returned. Qui-Gon consulted the readout and turned to Obi-Wan. His face was streaked with dust, his tunic stained and filthy. Obi-Wan knew he must look just the same.

"We must travel through the night again, Padawan. Can you do it?"

Obi-Wan had reached a place where his body did not feel fatigue. He knew it was there, deep in his muscles and bones, and that he would feel it once this pursuit was over. Until then, he would not allow himself.

"I can do it," he said.

Qui-Gon nodded and sped off. Again, they rode through the dark night. The cold air revived Obi-Wan and he took deep breaths of it to restore himself. The night streamed past in a blur of landscape and rising and setting moons.

The sky was just beginning to lighten when

the probe droid returned. It had taken less time for its reconnaissance. That could be a good sign. Obi-Wan kept his eyes on Qui-Gon as he quickly accessed the readout. When Qui-Gon turned, his eyes gleamed in satisfaction.

"He has stopped. The droid has just left him, so he'll be there this time. We've got him." He leaped off his speeder. "We must proceed carefully, Padawan. There is a small canyon just ahead. Balog is there."

They proceeded silently toward a rocky outcropping. Qui-Gon signaled, indicating that they would find Balog around the rocks.

They moved silently but speedily. The darkness was starting to lift, but there were still deep shadows cast by the rocks and cliffs around them. They moved into the shadows of the cliff. It would give them cover.

They climbed over some rocks and entered the canyon. Ahead they saw a small fire burning. There was no sign of Balog's hoverscout, but a figure lay near the fire, wrapped in a thermal quilt. Perhaps the hoverscout was parked nearby, deep in the shadows. Obi-Wan focused on the figure near the fire. Was it Balog? Or could it be Tahl?

Qui-Gon's steps slowed. He peered ahead through the dimness at the figure on the ground. He put out a hand to slow Obi-Wan down.

"Something is wrong," he muttered. "Can you feel it?"

Before Obi-Wan could respond, two dark shapes in the sky swooped down toward them. Probe droids.

And then Obi-Wan saw their own probe droid dart to the left, circling the canyon. He pointed it out to Qui-Gon, who looked up at it, puzzled, just as blaster fire ripped into the rocks behind them.

"It's a trap!" Qui-Gon shouted.

CHAPTER 6

Balog had fooled them. He was gone, but he had left two attack droids.

One of these droids peeled off and went after the Jedi's probe droid. The other headed for the Jedi.

Their droid shifted into attack mode from the threat. Blaster fire pinged overhead as the two droids found each other's positions and battled.

"We can't lose that droid," Qui-Gon said urgently. He activated his lightsaber and jumped behind a boulder for cover. "Obi-Wan, get back to your swoop. One of us needs to fight the droids from the air."

Obi-Wan hated to leave his Master, but he saw the wisdom of Qui-Gon's strategy. He sprinted toward his swoop. He could hear blaster fire erupt behind him, and had to discipline himself not to turn and check on Qui-Gon's safety. He had to trust his Master to handle the situation until his return.

The wind whistled past his ears as he raced across the terrain. He leaped onto his swoop and pushed the engines to maximum. He zoomed back toward the canyon.

Qui-Gon had jumped or climbed to a narrow ledge above the canyon floor. As the probe droid circled and dived, peppering Qui-Gon with blaster fire, Qui-Gon used his lightsaber in a series of quick defensive moves. Obi-Wan knew he was biding his time until the droid came closer, so he could leap toward it with his lightsaber. It was a waiting game.

"Get that other droid!" Qui-Gon shouted.

Obi-Wan wanted to protect Qui-Gon. But Qui-Gon was right. Losing a probe droid would drastically lower the odds of finding Tahl quickly.

He shot up to where the probe droids were battling and activated his lightsaber. It was hard, even from close range, to tell which droid was theirs.

Qui-Gon saw Obi-Wan's hesitation. "The one on the left, Padawan!" he called out.

Obi-Wan focused on the two droids, noting any nicks and scratches that would identify the one he needed to destroy. Balog's droid had a deep scratch on one side. Confident now, Obi-Wan moved closer, angling to take his first strike.

Balog's droid suddenly veered and dived, blasting fire at the Jedi droid. The droid took evasive action, blaster fire missing it by centimeters. Obi-Wan gunned the motor and leaned to the right, angling the swoop closer. His balance had to be perfect or the swoop would tumble end over end in midair. He made a sudden dive on top of Balog's droid, swiping with his lightsaber. But the droid had already reversed course, and he missed.

Obi-Wan righted the swoop and raced up toward the probe droid. He could not let the droid get another shot out. At the same time he had to stay out of his own droid's angle of fire.

Balog's probe droid veered again. Obi-Wan followed. There was only so much strategy a droid could have. Obi-Wan dived, anticipating the droid's move. At the same time, the Jedi droid fired at Balog's.

"To the left, Padawan!" Qui-Gon shouted.

Without looking, without thinking, Obi-Wan pulled the swoop to the left, barely missing blaster fire from his own droid. Instead of righting the swoop, he used the move to circle, then zoom up, coming at Balog's droid head on. He saw the red sensor blink as it computed his position. He had only seconds.

He rammed the engines into screaming full power and leaned off the swoop as far as he could, raising his lightsaber high. The lightsaber came down and cut the droid neatly in two. Sputtering and smoking, it fell to the ground below and crashed.

Obi-Wan turned the swoop again, this time heading for Balog's second droid. It had altered its flight plan to fly lower since it could not get a good reading on Qui-Gon. Obi-Wan kept to the droid's left, leaving Qui-Gon room to maneuver.

He glanced quickly at Qui-Gon, who nodded. They didn't need to compare notes; they had arrived at the same plan. Obi-Wan sent the swoop into a dive at the same time as Qui-Gon leaped. The two Jedi soared toward the droid, their lightsabers pulsating. Together, they timed their blows — Qui-Gon an upward sweep, Obi-Wan a downward thrust. The probe droid had no way to escape. It fell under both blows and disintegrated in a shower of metal and sparks.

But what Obi-Wan hadn't taken into account was their own probe droid. It had reprogrammed itself to attack the second droid, and fired at the same time.

Obi-Wan felt a warning surge in the Force and quickly accelerated. He was fast enough to avoid getting hit but not fast enough to bring the swoop completely out of danger. He heard blaster fire pepper the body of the swoop. Immediately it began to smoke and sputter. Obi-Wan carefully guided it toward the ground.

Qui-Gon landed on his feet. Obi-Wan pulled up next to him.

Qui-Gon's face was grimy and streaked with sweat as he looked impassively at the swoop.

"I'm sorry, Master," Obi-Wan said disgust-edly as he jumped off the damaged swoop. "Too much of my focus was on Balog's droid."

"It's all right," Qui-Gon said in his quietest voice. Obi-Wan knew the setback had upset him. "You did well. We still have our probe droid."

Qui-Gon bent to examine the swoop. Part of the control panel had fused together. After a moment he lifted his head. "It's worse than I thought. It will take some time to repair it. Or else we could leave it here. But then there will be no room to bring Tahl back . . ."

"Unless we capture Balog and his transport."

"Which we can't count on. Getting Tahl to safety is our first concern. We can't make an-other mistake."

Qui-Gon was still keeping his voice pitched low, but Obi-Wan could see the boiling frustra-tion in his eyes. He wished he could replay the fight. He wished he had remembered to watch out for their own droid.

"Go on without me, Master," he said. "I'll stay and repair the swoop and catch up to you."

"No," Qui-Gon said. "I won't leave you alone in this area. Lenz told me that it is dangerous. There are Worker supporters and Absolute loyalists who often meet in violent clashes. Besides, Tahl is too vulnerable. She is trapped, and if Balog gets one second free, he could inject her again and possibly kill her. We need to do this together."

"I'm sorry," Obi-Wan said again.

Qui-Gon put a hand on his shoulder. "Enough. It is a delay. Nothing more. Get the repair kit from the speeder. We are wasting time."

Obi-Wan ran back to the landspeeder, his heart pounding. Qui-Gon had said all the right things to reassure him, but he didn't feel any better. Repairing the swoop could take several hours. If this delay meant that Tahl was moved beyond their reach, he would feel responsible.

When he returned, he found Qui-Gon bent over the figure by the smoking fire. It was just a bundle of clothes wrapped in a thermal blanket. Qui-Gon extracted a sensor.

"This is what confused the droid," he said. "It's an infrared sensor. It thought Balog was still here. I had a feeling we would find this. It should have occurred to me earlier." Qui-Gon squinted at the empty landscape. "He knows we're following. When his probe droids fail to return, he'll know we won this battle. He will do something else to delay us. We must be on our guard."

CHAPTER 7

Qui-Gon sat in the star map room at the Temple. The soft blue light surrounded him. The planet holograms swirled around him in the fantastic array of colors the galaxy provided. This was his favorite room at the Temple, yet recently he had not been drawn here. It was such a quiet place, and Qui-Gon had sought to cure his restlessness with activity rather than calm.

The door opened and Tahl entered, then stopped abruptly. Although she could not see him, she knew he was there. Once, he had asked her how she knew him immediately — was it his breathing pattern, his scent, some betrayal of movement? She had only smiled. "It is just you," she'd said.

But there was no smile today. He and Tahl had been arguing or avoiding each other for months. Whenever he returned from a mission, he would go to see her, as he always had. But their conversations did not go well. Lately, their arguments had circled around Tahl's treatment of Bant, her new Padawan. She was a kind teacher and respected Bant's unique abilities, but she often left her behind and went on short missions on her own.

"I'm sorry," she said stiffly. "You came here to be alone."

So she could tell that, too. "Stay, please," he said.

She sat close to him, tucking her knees up to her chin in a pose he hadn't seen since she was a young girl. "I'm disturbing your refuge. Well, sometimes you need disturbing, Qui-Gon."

"No doubt."

"You know, your calmness can be infuriating," Tahl said. "But this moodiness is worse. I'm trying not to take it personally, but either you avoid me or you smother me with concern because of my blindness or you attack me about how I am with my Padawan. If you're trying to test our friendship, you're doing a very good job."

She spoke lightly, but he knew she meant it.

What could he say? She presented a good front to others. Her extraordinary compensations for her blindness had convinced everyone that she had come to terms with it. He knew the truth. He'd known her since she was a girl. Tahl was such an independent spirit. Now she disliked having to ask for help or guidance. Yet there were times she needed it.

"I'm only trying to look out for you," he said carefully. "Then when I do, you push me away."

"Why shouldn't I push you away when you crowd me? You should be used to me by now. You know I have to find my way. We all do. You've had more experience as a Master, it's true. But you also know that each Master finds a separate path with his or her Padawan."

"I do know that."

"Then why can't you let me find my own?"

The question hung between them. Qui-Gon realized he didn't know the answer. He was not one to interfere in other lives. A solitary man, he respected privacy. But with Tahl, it was different. He had a deep feeling that she needed protection, and he had been relieved when she had chosen Bant as her Padawan. But Tahl would not depend on Bant to help her, either.

Her friendship was the most important thing. He needed to back off.

"You're right," he said. "I was wrong."

"Stars and galaxies," she murmured. "I wasn't expecting an apology. I was expecting another argument."

"Well, there are things I could say —"

She smacked his knee. "I know that. How about we just be quiet, for once? We can't get into trouble that way."

So Qui-Gon sat with her, watching the hologram planets whirl. For the first time in weeks, he felt at peace. Strange how her quiet presence could soothe as well as irritate him.

It had been their last quiet time together. The next morning, he found out she was going on a quick mission to the rough satellite planet Vandor 3. She was leaving Bant behind. By the morning meal, they were arguing again.

The delay caused by the damage to the swoop made them push themselves even harder. The new coordinates the probe droid brought back spurred them on. By the next morning they had reached the vast rock quarries of New Apsolon, where the gray stone that had been used to build the majority of the buildings in the capital city was harvested.

It was rough country, with vast boulders, cliffs, and deep pits, some filled with water. A good place to hide, Qui-Gon thought. Perhaps they were approaching Balog's destination.

Obi-Wan had been silent for hours, his face drawn. Qui-Gon knew his Padawan still felt badly about the delay. He had no more words of reassurance for him. Obi-Wan would have to look forward, like a Jedi. His Padawan knew that Qui-Gon was frantic to find Tahl, but most likely thought his zeal to find her had to do with their long friendship. He did not know how much of Qui-Gon's spirit was bound up in Tahl's safety. He could not know how full Qui-Gon's heart was, and how difficult that made it for him to speak.

All will be well, Qui-Gon told himself, *when I find her. When I see her. When I know she is safe . . .*

Qui-Gon wrenched his mind away from the future. It had been worrying him, how often his thoughts went to his reunion with Tahl. It sprang from his need to see her safe. Yet it was dangerous for him to dwell on the future, he knew. Balog was still ahead of them. That was all he needed to know. His attention must be on each present moment. His focus was distracted, and he could be missing things as he traveled. He was not thinking like a Jedi. How could he teach his Padawan when he himself had trouble reaching his calm center?

Qui-Gon drew his focus around him. His hands remained steady on the controls of the landspeeder. His progress continued. Yet he directed his concentration away from his piloting to take in the landscape around him, the Force vibrating, present as it was always present, teaching him as it always taught him.

Then he felt it. A flicker of something . . . danger, perhaps. He might have noticed it before. It might have been lurking underneath the surface of his worry for some time. It was a separate worry from his distress over Tahl. Now he examined it fully, turning it over in his mind. A ripple in the Force, an undercurrent, a warning. A different energy was behind them.

Someone was tailing them.

He did not say anything to Obi-Wan. He cast his focus back, alert for any clue. They drove on.

By dusk, he was certain. They were gaining on Balog now. The last report from the droid told them that their ability to go long periods without sleep had helped them. Balog had stopped, and stopped again. The distance was closing. This time, Qui-Gon believed it because he could feel it.

Yet the fact that someone was behind them could impede their progress. He sensed that this being was gaining on them. He or she was close now. If they were overtaken and attacked, they could lose precious time.

It was time to tell Obi-Wan.

"There is someone behind us, following us," Qui-Gon said the next time they stopped to check their position. "I think it might be better to circle back and surprise them before they surprise us. I don't like the delay, but it would be better in the long run to deal with this."

"I didn't sense anything," Obi-Wan said unhappily.

"It was a suggestion, nothing more. Very faint, but it grew. Don't dwell on your lapse, Obi-Wan. Look forward. This is a good lesson. Even in pursuit, your focus should be a wide circle, taking in everything around you."

Obi-Wan nodded. "Do you have any ideas about who it could be?"

Qui-Gon shook his head. "I wouldn't guess."

"It could be Irini," Obi-Wan said. "She seemed very anxious about that list."

"It could also be a comrade of Balog's," Qui-Gon said. "If Balog knows we're gaining on him, he might call for help. I don't want to use the probe droid to track our pursuer. We're going to have to do it ourselves."

"I'm ready," Obi-Wan agreed.

They turned back, making a wide circle to avoid being seen. Qui-Gon pointed ahead to a cluster of hill formations formed from solid rock. He gestured that they should go around them. He remembered that they had gone through the formation in the center, where a rough passage was cut through the rock. He had a feeling their pursuer was inside that narrow passage. It was a good place for them to ambush whoever it was.

They zoomed around the formation, then headed into the passage, moving at top speed now. Ahead, Qui-Gon saw the reverberations of a fast-moving landspeeder. He motioned to Obi-Wan, and Obi-Wan guided his repaired swoop high in the air. Qui-Gon pushed the engines faster as Obi-Wan zoomed above. Within seconds, they were on top of the other transport.

Their pursuer looked back in surprise. A gold braid whipped around in the wind, slapping her in the cheek.

It was one of the twins — at this speed, Qui-Gon couldn't tell which one.

The twin stopped her landspeeder and leaped off. Qui-Gon slowed his own engine. Obi-Wan landed the swoop. As she strode toward them, he saw it was Eritha. He was surprised. Alani had been the more forceful of the twins. Eritha tended to stay in the background. Why had she come on this rugged journey?

"I'm so glad to find you!" she cried. "I've been traveling for days. I didn't know how to reach you. I found out who is backing Balog. I know who your enemy is."

"Who?" Qui-Gon asked.

Eritha hesitated a moment. Her lips pressed together in a thin line, as if she were reluctant to let the words out. "My sister," she said.

CHAPTER 8

"Alani is in contact with Balog," Eritha continued. The words now tumbled out of her. "I heard her speaking to him on a comlink. I couldn't tell where he was, or where he was headed. Tahl is alive, but he's keeping her contained in that horrible device."

Tahl is alive. Obi-Wan saw the relief transform Qui-Gon's face before his Master turned his full attention back to Eritha again.

"Do you see what this means?" Eritha cried. She twisted her hands together. "Alani must have lied to me all along! She convinced me that Roan was behind our father's death. And I'm sure that she engineered our own kidnapping." She went on angrily. "No wonder she was so strong during the ordeal. After we were released, I was afraid they were tracking us to kill us. She kept telling me not to be afraid, not to worry. . . ." Eritha's voice was full of disgust. "I thought she was so brave. And Roan — could she have arranged to kill Roan? I can't believe that! He was so kind to us. He was our father's best friend!"

"What is her goal?" Obi-Wan asked.

"Power. She wants to rule New Apsolon." Eritha shook her head. "At least that's what I think they are planning. Balog will back her along with the Absolutes. I can't believe what I'm saying. I can't believe I never knew my sister. I'm so ashamed."

"But you didn't do anything wrong," Obi-Wan said.

"Don't you understand? She is part of me. I should have known." Eritha's gaze was bleak.

"Are you sure she gave no clues to Balog's whereabouts?" Qui-Gon asked urgently.

Eritha sighed woefully. "I'm sorry. I overheard the conversation, but they never mentioned where he was."

"Thank you for coming and telling us this," Qui-Gon said. "You risked much. Now you must return."

"I'm not going back." Eritha's jaw set stubbornly, removing the softness that distinguished her from her more dynamic and electric sister.

"I am sorry," Qui-Gon said firmly, "but you must. Obi-Wan and I are going ahead. It will be dangerous."

"I don't care. My sister has shamed my planet. I must restore my family's honor. She is a Worker and has betrayed the Workers by making an alliance with the Absolutes. Do you see what this means? She thinks that because of who her father is, the Workers will accept her without question. Even as we speak she is maneuvering to get the United Legislature to appoint her as Supreme Governor. I know how she is doing it, too — I know her. She won't ask, she won't suggest. She'll be sweet and modest. Somehow those high up in the Legislature will think they came up with the idea on their own. Just as she once made me believe that Roan was involved in Ewane's death. Of course the Workers will support her — she is a heroine, for surviving our father's death.

"Once appointed, she will bring back the Absolutes and slowly restore the government to what it was. The Workers will be trampled. No." Eritha crossed her arms. "I will not return. My dead father is at my shoulder. He sacrificed too much. I am coming with you."

"Eritha, we think Balog is probably heading to his supporters. You are not trained for battle," Obi-Wan said.

"Oh, but I am." Eritha drew back her cloak, exposing the blasters and explosive devices on her belt. "I have excellent aim."

"I admire your dedication," Qui-Gon said. "However —"

"Tahl was a great friend to me when I needed one," Eritha said, staring Qui-Gon down. "I can't desert her now. And you forget that I have been through the same thing. I was trapped in that device. I know what it does to you. I have to do this, Qui-Gon."

Qui-Gon was about to speak, but suddenly an explosion shattered the rocks at their side. Shards flew out at them. Both Obi-Wan and Qui-Gon sprang forward to protect Eritha. Qui-Gon shielded her with his body while they leaped behind her speeder.

"Keep your head down," Qui-Gon ordered sternly. "It looks as though our battle has found us."

CHAPTER 9

It wasn't Balog who was attacking. After the dust cleared, Qui-Gon and Obi-Wan caught a glimpse of a group of beings who blended in with the rocks and dirt. They wore gray unisuits and their skin was the same ashy color. They moved from boulder to boulder, trying to close in on the Jedi.

Obi-Wan saw a thin beam of light pulse over their heads toward the canyon wall. "Move back!" he shouted to Qui-Gon and Eritha.

They jumped back just seconds before a slide of rock and shale landed where they had been.

"They're using a beamdrill to create rock slides," Obi-Wan said.

Qui-Gon looked behind them. "They most likely are driving us into an ambush."

"What should we do?" Eritha asked. Her face was taut, her eyes wide with fear.

Another pulse hit the rock face, and the three

jumped back in time to avoid another shuddering explosion of rock. The shards flew toward them, and they covered their heads until the dust settled.

"We need to get above the range of the beamdrill," Qui-Gon said, scanning the canyon wall. "If we can get on top of the rock, they can't follow us."

"Our cable launchers don't go that high," Obi-Wan said. "We'll have to keep relaunching."

"And meanwhile they'll still be using that beamdrill," Eritha said.

"I think it's our only chance," Qui-Gon decided. "Stay close," he warned Eritha.

She shuddered. "Don't worry."

"Qui-Gon! Our probe droid is approaching!" Obi-Wan called.

"We need better cover!" Eritha shouted, panicked. She darted forward suddenly as the beamdrill pulse hit an area over their heads.

As rocks began to rain down, Qui-Gon leaped toward Eritha to bring her to safety. Obi-Wan followed, activating his lightsaber to deflect the rocks from the probe droid.

Qui-Gon grabbed Eritha and landed safely behind a pile of debris. Obi-Wan wasn't as lucky. He was seconds too late to save the probe droid. A large boulder hit the droid straight on, shattering it. Obi-Wan barely had time to register this before he realized a shower of rocks was headed toward him. He twisted in midair, but a large rock caught him in the leg. He fell, and his leg gave way underneath him.

"Stay here!" Qui-Gon roared to Eritha, pushing her head down. He raced forward, picked Obi-Wan up in his arms, and with a mighty leap, landed beyond the safety of the new pile of rocks the attack had created.

"Master . . . the droid . . . I'm sorry . . ." Obi-Wan's breath came in gasps. His leg throbbed.

Qui-Gon felt the leg gently. "It's not broken. After you catch your breath you might be able to stand on it. If not, I'll carry you."

Obi-Wan nodded. He gathered himself to accept the pain, to open himself to the Force so he could begin to heal.

They were almost at the end of the narrow canyon. Obi-Wan knew he would not be able to use his cable launcher to get above the beam-drills. By the grim look on Qui-Gon's face, he knew his Master had already realized this and was formulating another plan.

Suddenly two explosions went off farther down the narrow passage, and a rock slide began, larger than the ones before. Qui-Gon and Obi-Wan covered their heads.

When they were able to see through the choking dust, the end of the canyon was blocked off by a towering pile of rock and rubble.

"We're trapped," Obi-Wan said.

Qui-Gon activated his lightsaber. "They still have to come and get us. And we have the cover of the landslides they've already created."

They heard a grinding noise, and a mole miner appeared at the other end of the canyon. The utility vehicle lumbered toward them slowly.

"Mole miners can bore through solid rock," Obi-Wan said. "Our cover is about to disintegrate."

Just then Eritha dashed over to them from behind her own cover. "What is that?" she asked Qui-Gon.

"A mole miner," Qui-Gon said. "It's a utility craft used by miners."

"So our attackers are miners?" Eritha asked.

"I'd say yes," Qui-Gon said. "So far they've used mining equipment to attack us. Maybe they don't have conventional weapons."

"That could be good news," Eritha muttered. Suddenly, she scrambled over the rock pile.

"Eritha!" Qui-Gon yelled, reaching for her.

She jumped from the top of the pile to the ground. Then she threw back the hood of her cloak and raised her hands.

"Stay here, Padawan." Qui-Gon leaped over

the rock pile in one fluid motion. He stood with his lightsaber activated, ready to defend Eritha.

"Put away your weapon, Qui-Gon," Eritha said through her teeth. "And trust me."

The mole miner advanced a few meters, then stopped.

Slowly, Qui-Gon deactivated his lightsaber. Obi-Wan watched, knowing his Master could still attack in a movement faster than the eye could see.

Slowly, a hatch opened at the top of the mole miner. A ramp emerged. A man and a woman crawled out and walked down the ramp.

They faced Qui-Gon and Eritha and bowed.

"Daughter of Ewane, we are at your service," the man said. Obi-Wan now saw that their skin was gray with rock dust.

Eritha bowed in return. "I am Eritha."

The tall woman spoke. "We thought you were a team from the Absolutes. We apologize. They have been raiding our settlements and stealing supplies."

"Who are you?" Qui-Gon asked.

"We are the Rock Workers. We are allies of the Tech Workers in the city. We are glad to see that you were not harmed."

"But we were," Qui-Gon said. "My Padawan

is hurt. And our probe droid was destroyed. It was tracking an Absolute."

"Then we are truly sorry," the man said, distressed. "If you come with us to our settlement, we have excellent med care. We will help you any way we can."

CHAPTER 10

The air was so crisp and clear on Ragoon-6 that it gave you the feeling you could see to the future, or back to the past. Tahl had proposed the training exercise to Qui-Gon on one of their rare meetings at the Temple. If they did not take the time now, when would they? she had pointed out, her chin thrusting at him as it did when she wanted her own way. Soon they would both be sent on missions again.

He knew that she had proposed the trip because of what had happened with Xanatos. His Padawan had turned to the dark side, and weeks of meditation and talks with Yoda had not reconciled Qui-Gon to that. He sensed that Yoda was concerned about his progress. Yet he was stuck, thinking over and over about everything he had done and everything he should have done.

To his relief, Tahl hadn't brought up Xanatos once on Ragoon-6. Instead they had concentrated on the exercise. The landscape of Ragoon-6 was breathtaking, but it was difficult terrain. They pushed their bodies to the limit as they scaled mountains and hiked rocky trails.

They paused to rest on a flat rock overlooking a deep valley.

"Do you see that flying irid?" Tahl said, pointing. "Look at the yellow on the underside of its wings."

Qui-Gon looked where she pointed. Tahl could always see farther than he could. He waited until his eyes could track the bird, a flash of brilliant color in the blue sky. "Beautiful."

"Yes. But they are horrible birds. They attack their own kind. It's strange, though. They nurture their young with great care. They teach them to fly, to hunt, to nest. Yet when their young reach maturity they are just as likely to eat their parents as each other."

Qui-Gon stared out at the valley. "Are parables supposed to make me feel better? I know you are talking about Xanatos. I nurtured him and he betrayed me. It was not my fault. It was his nature. Is that what you're saying?"

"I'm talking about irids," Tahl said composedly. "But now that you brought him up —"

"Excuse me, I didn't —"

"I'd like to make one point. You can't control everything you touch, Qui-Gon. And you can't make sense of everything, either, no matter how much you analyze or meditate. Not even you."

"This is not about ego," he said.

She shot him a keen look, all emerald and gold. "Isn't it?"

Another delay. Qui-Gon wanted to bellow his rage to the sky. Instead, he helped his Padawan to Eritha's landspeeder and gently lowered him into the seat. Obi-Wan's face was drawn with pain.

The last thing he wanted to do right now was take a detour from their quest, but his Padawan needed care.

Eritha drove her landspeeder, and a Rock Worker took Obi-Wan's swoop. Qui-Gon followed as they raced through the canyons toward the Rock Workers' settlement.

He was glad that the distance wasn't far. The

settlement lay in a small valley surrounded by quarries. Walkways made of slate were laid out in rows and led to residences, stores, a school, and a small med unit.

Obi-Wan was met by a young woman who hurried out immediately to look at his wound.

"I am a trained medic," she said. "My name is Yanci. I've seen many wounds such as this in the quarries. This isn't too bad. Your friend will mend quickly."

Qui-Gon nodded his thanks. Together he and Yanci helped Obi-Wan into the med center.

"I can take over from here," Yanci told him, setting out a splint and beginning the procedure for a bacta bath. "The refreshment unit is across the walkway. Why don't you rest, and I will come over and give you a progress report?"

Obi-Wan flashed Qui-Gon a grin that was also a grimace. "I'm fine here."

Qui-Gon patted his shoulder in support, then left the med unit. It might be helpful to talk to the Rock Workers about the Absolutes. He was surprised to hear that the Absolutes had been conducting raids. That meant their numbers were bigger than he'd thought. That was most likely not good news for his mission. He felt frustration rise up and threaten to choke him. He took a deep breath to calm himself. The frustration eased, but he knew it still simmered, ready to boil again. He wanted to continue tracking, but he couldn't leave Obi-Wan without knowing the extent of his injury.

Qui-Gon walked across to the refreshment unit. There he found the two Rock Workers who had been inside the mole miner. They had brought tea and food to Eritha. Qui-Gon shook his head at their offer as he took a seat opposite them.

The tall female pointed to her companion. "I am Bini, and this is Kevta," she said. "Again, we must tell you how sorry we are to have mistaken you for Absolutes. We don't get travelers out in this area, so we jumped to conclusions too fast. How is your young friend?"

"It was an understandable mistake," Qui-Gon said. "Obi-Wan will be fine, according to your medic. She'll give me a report soon."

"Yanci has great skill. It is good that you brought him here."

"Tell me," Qui-Gon said. "You said that the Absolutes had raided your camp. How many were there?"

Kevta stirred honey into his tea. "We were attacked by a squad of maybe thirty, but when there are casualties, more take their place. We have no way of knowing. We are forty here, but that includes elders and children. The Absolutes are also heavily armed. In the first raid, they captured our small weapons — blasters and flechette missiles."

"You don't know where their headquarters are?" he pressed.

Bini cupped her mug of tea in her hands. Qui-Gon noted that her hands were large and looked extraordinarily strong. One finger was black and blue, and there were old scars on her knuckles. Her hands told him how hard the work conditions were at the quarries better than words could.

"We do not know," she said quietly. "We have searched. If they have a base, it is well hidden."

Qui-Gon felt his irritation rise. There was so little information to be had. He couldn't get over the feeling that he was wasting time. "Is it possible that they conduct their raids from the city?"

Kevta shook his head. "No. We know their base is in the quarries somewhere. Their raids are spaced too close. Especially lately. We have been raided five times in the past month."

"Do you have weapons left?" Qui-Gon asked.

"We have a few blasters, not many," Kevta said. "We only have our tools and the explosives we use in the quarries. They are expensive and we don't like to use them. But we are getting desperate. That is why we attacked you today. We have had enough. We know they are after our large explosives. If we lose those, we're doomed. This mining outfit is a cooperative. We all share in the work and profits. If we lose our tools and explosives, we won't be able to buy more."

"You need help," Eritha said. "Have you informed the United Legislature? They could send a security force to protect you."

"We informed them weeks ago and have heard nothing," Bini said. "The troubles in the capital city have overshadowed ours."

Qui-Gon thought over what Bini and Kevta had told him. He remembered back to Mota, the black market seller with the empty tables where weapons had once been for sale. The Absolutes were gathering weapons on a large scale. They were ready to make their move. All of this had coincided with Tahl's kidnapping. But was there a connection?

Restlessly, Qui-Gon drummed his fingers on the table, then stilled them. Eritha watched him over the rim of her mug.

The door opened, and Yanci strode in. She saw Qui-Gon immediately and came over.

"Obi-Wan is a good patient," she said, "only stubborn. He wants to leave. But I am prevailing on you to reason with him. His wound will heal, but he needs time for the bacta to regenerate what he lost."

"How long?" Qui-Gon asked.

"A day. Maybe more. He will risk permanent damage if he does not stay off that leg."

Qui-Gon nodded. Accepting the diagnosis was not easy. Every part of him was screaming to leave, to rescue Tahl. He should at least wait until morning before making a decision. He wanted to leave tonight. Right now.

Yanci seemed to understand. "The moons are waning. It would be difficult to track tonight. The quarries are treacherous."

"Do you have a probe droid you can lend us?"

Bini shook her head. "Probe droids are illegal. Absolutes still use them, of course. We do not."

Qui-Gon saw he had no choice. Reluctantly, he rose. "May I sleep in the med unit tonight? I don't want Obi-Wan to be alone."

"I'll make arrangements," Yanci promised.

"And Eritha can sleep in my unit," Bini said.

"It is only one more day," Yanci said.

But one more day could mean everything. He could not risk Obi-Wan's health. Qui-Gon pushed his decision off until morning. If Obi-Wan was not better, he would consider going on alone and leave Eritha here with him. It was not a choice he wanted to make.

And when the chase began again, he would not have the probe droid. He would have to track Balog on his own. It would take longer. He might not succeed.

Tahl felt farther away than ever.

Be strong, Tahl. You pledged your life to me. I gave you my heart. Know that I will find you.

CHAPTER 11

Now that Qui-Gon had just become a Jedi Knight, Yoda had suggested it was time he took a Padawan. Qui-Gon decided to go on one last mission while he thought about it. He never did anything rashly. He had a Padawan in mind, and it was easier to consider him away from the Temple.

He had a stopover in Zekulae while he waited for transport. It was a barren world, noted for its mineral soil, which was dark and rich and studded with blue crystals. The soil was so fine that within days it was everywhere — in his hair, in his mouth, in his boots. Qui-Gon found that his careful thoughts about his future had shrunk to a longing for his next shower.

He stopped in a café for a cool drink. He sipped it, eyeing the locals. Zekulae was not overly dangerous, but you had to be careful here. The government had a relaxed attitude toward rules and laws. Disputes were most often settled with fists or blasters.

Suddenly an argument broke out behind him. It was between two beings playing sabacc. One was a native of Zekulae, the other hidden by a column. The Zeku stood, scattering the cards.

"Strange that you're the one so upset, when I'm the one who's been cheated," a dry voice said.

Qui-Gon knew the voice, even though it had changed. He hadn't heard it in years. It was deeper, huskier than he remembered.

Tahl rose from the table. He waited, watching her, as did everyone in the café. She commanded attention. He didn't know her mission here. It might not be safe if she were seen talking to a Jedi. She was wearing a traveler's cloak and boots, and her lightsaber was hidden.

The Zeku moved his hand toward his belt, but he didn't get a chance to draw his weapon. Within the space of an eye blink, Tahl reached out and disarmed him, at the same time pressing one shoulder so that he was forced to sit back down in his chair, hard. Maintaining the pressure, she scooped some credits off the table.

"Let's call it even," she said. "And I'll buy you a drink. Wouldn't you rather live to see the sunset?"

He nodded, his face contorted in pain. She called to the bartender. "Something special for my friend here."

She tucked the credits inside her tunic, released the Zeku, and walked on. Nobody in the café moved. No one spoke. They all watched the woman who combined elegance and danger walk casually through them.

Qui-Gon watched her, too, admiring her toughness and grace. He was astonished at how lovely she was. Her extraordinary eyes and the strength of her features had become dramatic and striking with maturity.

Then she saw him, and her face lost its severe cast. She came over to his table and sat as conversations started up around them. The incident was over.

"Well, it's you," she said. "It's been so long."

"Too long."

"I only have a minute," she said. "I'm on a mission."

Only a minute, when they hadn't seen each other in years!

"So tell me everything as fast as you

can," she said, laughing. "You look well. I hear you are now a Knight."

"As are you," Qui-Gon said. "I'm thinking of taking a Padawan. Yoda is urging me to consider it."

"Do you have a candidate?"

"Xanatos."

She nodded slowly. "He is gifted. I would consider carefully, however. I'm not sure he's the right one for you."

"I haven't seen you in years, and you're giving me advice?" he teased.

"Who else in the galaxy understands you so well?" she answered, smiling.

"No one," he admitted. "You were wrong about that. Remember what you said when we said good-bye?"

Her smile grew soft. "I am glad," she said, "to have been wrong about that. I'm glad to still be the one who knows you best. And we never said good-bye. Remember?"

They sat for a moment in silence, remembering the Temple, the days when they had looked forward so eagerly to becoming Jedi Knights. They hadn't known then how hard it would turn out to be. Neither had they known how deeply satisfying it would be at the same time. Yes, a life of service suited him. Suited Tahl, he could see. And it *was something, to have this connection now, still so strong after so many years.*

"I have to go," she said softly. "I will see you soon. Missions can be short, you know."

He smiled, remembering the eager, young Tahl who had said that so confidently years ago.

She stood. She did not say good-bye. He knew she wouldn't, no more than she ever said hello. With a last smile, she walked out of the café and did not look back.

Dusk fell quickly. Qui-Gon checked on Obi-Wan and found him in deep meditation. He quietly went out again, glad to see it. Obi-Wan was focusing his mind on healing. Maybe his Padawan would be ready to travel by morning. He had no doubts as to Yanci's diagnostic abilities, but she had never treated a Jedi before.

Qui-Gon strolled through the Rock Workers' settlement, taking deep breaths of the cool night air. He was impressed with its design and organization. He could see that though the quarry work was difficult, the Workers themselves had created a good life. They took care of each other and their young. Under other circumstances, he would have enjoyed the brief stop. Now he only wanted to be gone.

He found Yanci, Bini, and Kevta sitting outside a small housing unit, and they waved him over.

"We were enjoying the stars," Kevta said. "It is a hard life out here, but I tried city work. It didn't take."

"I'm glad to have run into you," Qui-Gon said, settling himself beside them. "Would you mind if I asked you more questions about the raids? It might help us track the Absolutes."

"We will tell you what we can," Kevta said.

"I think I'll make sure Eritha is settled," Yanci said, rising. "Bini and Kevta are the strategists here." Qui-Gon noted how her hand lingered on Kevta's shoulder. He gave her a gentle smile as she left.

Qui-Gon questioned Bini and Kevta closely. By listening to the details, he was able to find a pattern in the direction of the attacks and the minimal amount of tracking the Rock Workers had done.

He left the two of them and walked slowly back to the med unit. Without knowing it, Bini and Kevta had given him good news. The Jedi did not have to return to their last coordinates. They could track Balog from a point a few kilometers from the Worker settlement. If Balog was heading to the Absolute camp, they should find some evidence of his route. There were only a few possible routes through the canyons.

Of course, it all depended on whether Balog was heading for the secret hideout of the Absolutes.

It was a chance they had to take.

Qui-Gon checked on Obi-Wan, who was now sleeping deeply. Good. Qui-Gon needed to do the same. It had been days since his last sleep. He quieted his mind, allowing sleep to come. He knew he had to operate at his peak, and his body told him that he needed rest.

He slept, but his dreams were vivid and disturbing. Once again he was in the café on Zekulae. His heart lifted at the sound of Tahl's voice. He rushed forward to greet her. But her gaze was lifeless, her eyes a dull black color. He realized she could not move or speak.

He woke with a start, his heart pounding. It was still dark, but dawn was near. He immediately swung his legs over his sleep couch and went to check on Obi-Wan. Obi-Wan seemed to feel his gaze. His eyes opened slowly, and then he came awake at once.

He tested his leg muscles, stretching beneath the thermal blanket.

"Better," he said.

He swung his legs over his sleep couch.

"Take it easy," Qui-Gon said. "Yanci thinks you need one more day."

Obi-Wan slid out of bed, holding one hand

against the wall to steady himself. He walked around the room. "Much better," he said. "I am ready to travel."

Qui-Gon studied his Padawan to make sure he was telling the truth. He knew Obi-Wan's desire to move on would be greater than his concern for himself. But his color was good, and there was no sign of pain on his face. His gait was a bit stiff, but it was steady.

"We'll see what Yanci says," he said.

When Yanci arrived, bringing Obi-Wan and Qui-Gon's breakfast, she was startled at Obi-Wan's recovery.

"I guess I'm better than even I thought," she said cheerfully. "I see no reason why you can't travel, Obi-Wan. Just try to rest the leg when you can, and apply bacta again tonight."

Qui-Gon left Obi-Wan finishing breakfast while Yanci added some items to his medpac. The suns were just a suggestion of orange along the horizon as Qui-Gon hurried to the speeders. They would need to be refueled before they took off. Every moment counted. And he should awaken Eritha. Part of him wanted to let her sleep so that they could leave her behind. He knew she would insist on coming with them, and he worried about her safety. Tahl was his first concern. Protecting Eritha would be a distraction he didn't need. But if he did not wake her, undoubtedly she would try to find them, and she could get into more trouble that way.

To his surprise, he found Eritha at the pen where their transports were kept.

"You're up early," he said.

She jumped. "You startled me."

"Obi-Wan is better."

She nodded. "I thought he would be. I came to start the refueling. I didn't want you to leave without me."

"I thought about it," Qui-Gon said. "Then I thought about how stubborn you are."

"It's a family trait." Eritha hesitated. "Tahl is important to me, Qui-Gon. I'd do anything for her. I promise I won't slow you down."

"I'll hold you to that," he said.

They completed the refueling in companionable silence, and Obi-Wan joined them. The stars had faded but the sky was still gray as they bid good-bye to Bini, Kevta, and Yanci.

Qui-Gon thanked them for their courtesy, but his mind was already on the day ahead. The tracking would not be easy.

"We wish you luck on your quest," Bini said.

"Don't push yourself with that leg," Yanci told Obi-Wan.

Obi-Wan thanked her and swung his leg a bit awkwardly over the saddle of his swoop. Eritha fired up her engines, and Qui-Gon took the lead.

With a last wave, they headed out of the settlement.

Qui-Gon went to the coordinates where the Rock Workers had lost the Absolute attack team the last time they pursued them.

"We need to find an indication that Balog headed this way as well," he told Obi-Wan. "The Rock Workers think the Absolutes took the west route through the canyons. Balog would have to change direction here."

"I don't understand," Eritha said. "The ground is sheer rock. How can you see anything?"

But the ground wasn't sheer rock, not to a Jedi. Obi-Wan left his swoop and began to search in ever-widening circles with Qui-Gon. Qui-Gon could see that his Padawan's leg was troubling him, but he focused on the task.

Obi-Wan found the first clue. At first it appeared to be a mere discoloration on rock. But further study told them it was the mark of Balog's high-speed engine. They recognized it now.

Qui-Gon crouched over the markings on the rock. "Good work, Padawan. Balog is heading west. Look at the pattern of the exhaust. That way." Qui-Gon pointed to the crags in the distance. Beyond the crags, he would find her. He could feel it. Her presence suddenly pulsed inside him like a heartbeat.

Eritha watched them, mystified and impressed.

"Remind me never to hide from the two of you," she said.

They set off again. Without the help of the probe droid, it was slow going. They were forced to dismount time after time to check their progress. By midday, they had found the campsite where Balog had spent the night.

"He left this morning," Qui-Gon said quietly, studying the flat rock where Balog had placed his condenser unit for heat. He could see a scorch mark and some boot marks in the surrounding dirt. "We are close." His gaze was fierce when he lifted his head. He looked past Obi-Wan toward the rugged landscape. "Very close."

Obi-Wan and Qui-Gon heard the noise of the transport at the same time. They both turned toward the source of the sound.

"What is it?" Eritha asked.

The speck in the distance grew rapidly and turned into Yanci, her auburn hair flying in the wind as she piloted a swoop at maximum speed toward them.

"Something's wrong," Obi-Wan said.

Yanci pulled up so rapidly she almost tipped the swoop. She hovered next to them.

"We need you," she gasped, out of breath. "A raid . . . a massive raid . . . like nothing we've seen —"

She bent over, trying to catch her breath. "This time they are trying to destroy the entire camp," she said after a moment. "They are killing as many of us as they can. Using small explosives and blasters. We have rallied who we can and have made a last stand in an out-building. We have some weapons. Not many."

Eritha put her hands to her cheeks. "This is terrible. We must do something."

"Of course we will come," Obi-Wan said.

"Padawan," Qui-Gon said. "May I speak with you." He turned to Yanci. "Just one moment, no more."

Obi-Wan dismounted from his swoop and went to join Qui-Gon a short distance away where they could not be overheard.

"You must return with Yanci," Qui-Gon told him. "I will go on. We are too close to Tahl to turn back."

Obi-Wan stared at him, astonished. Qui-Gon understood how he felt. The Rock Workers were in desperate need of help. The Jedi were asked to give it. He could not believe that Qui-Gon would turn away like this. But how could he return when he felt Tahl's presence, when he knew she was only hours away?

"It's hard to leave our pursuit of Tahl," Obi-Wan said. "But the Rock Workers need us, Qui-Gon."

"They need Jedi help, it is true," Qui-Gon said. He put his hand on Obi-Wan's shoulder. "You can provide this. But our first mission is to save Tahl."

"Our first mission always is to save lives and promote justice," Obi-Wan said, incredulous. "The Rock Workers need both of us, Qui-Gon."

"I am going forward," Qui-Gon said. His gaze was as flinty as the rocks surrounding them. "I cannot turn back now." Tahl was close. He could feel her. And he could feel that she was slipping away from him.

"What about Eritha?" Obi-Wan asked, lowering his voice. "If she returns with me, we will be putting her in danger. And if she goes on with you, she will not have the full protection she needs."

Obi-Wan was right. Qui-Gon struggled with the dilemma for a moment. "She will go with you," he said. "But before you reach the Rock Workers' camp, you must leave her in a safe place. You must do this, Obi-Wan. She has no place in that battle. I will come when I can."

"Master," Obi-Wan said, his eyes locking on Qui-Gon's, "this is wrong. You know it is. Tahl would say the same. How can you turn your back on these people?"

"Our mission is too important," Qui-Gon said.

"And Tahl . . ." His voice died away, and his hand dropped from Obi-Wan's shoulder.

They stood not speaking for a moment. Qui-Gon felt the gulf between them. His Padawan was filled with doubt and confusion. But he couldn't explain, not here, not now. He would have to go back to the vision he had on Coruscant, how every event since they'd arrived on New Apsolon had confirmed his dread. And he would have to tell Obi-Wan how he felt about Tahl. That was a conversation for another time.

His Padawan looked so confused that he relented. "Obi-Wan, I cannot abandon her," he said, his voice low. His gaze pleaded with Obi-Wan to understand.

But he got no such understanding. Obi-Wan shook his head. "You're wrong."

The flat words took him aback. It had been years since Obi-Wan had contradicted him so boldly. Qui-Gon flushed with an emotion he wasn't sure of himself.

He turned away without another word and headed to his landspeeder.

CHAPTER 12

With a grace surprising for a large man, Qui-Gon quickly sprang into the pilot seat, reversed the engines to turn the craft, and zoomed off.

Eritha ran toward Obi-Wan. "Qui-Gon isn't coming with us?"

"He has gone on with our mission," Obi-Wan said. "We will return with Yanci. But you will remain hidden outside the Rock Worker camp. You will not get involved in this battle."

He spoke the words automatically, his eyes on Qui-Gon's transport as it dwindled in the distance. He wondered if Qui-Gon had formulated a plan of attack for when they caught up to Balog. He assumed so. Yet Qui-Gon seemed so driven, so caught up in finding Balog, it did not seem he had time to formulate a strategy. Obi-Wan had wanted to ask, but did not want to insult his Master. Usually, Qui-Gon found his own time to inform Obi-Wan what he was thinking.

But Qui-Gon had not found that time. Obi-Wan was just as confused as when they'd started. Now Qui-Gon was violating Jedi principles by ignoring a cry for help.

He had spoken bluntly to his Master, but he did not regret his words. He was right. It was Qui-Gon's duty as a Jedi to turn away from what he wanted in order to help those who needed him.

Obi-Wan had felt this way once before, long ago, on the planet of Melida/Daan. There he had begged Qui-Gon to stay and help the Young. They were being massacred by their own leaders and parents. That day, Qui-Gon had refused to help in the same way. And Tahl had been the reason then, too.

Something in Obi-Wan's face prevented the argument that rose to Eritha's lips. Instead, she pressed them together and nodded. "I'll do what you say."

Relieved that he had won that battle, at least, Obi-Wan signaled to Yanci.

"Qui-Gon has to go on, but I am coming with you," he told her. "We need to find a place close to the camp to conceal Eritha."

"I know a place," Yanci said, nodding. She swung a leg over her swoop and waited for Obi-Wan and Eritha to mount their vehicles. Then, taking the lead, she sped off.

Obi-Wan felt his muscles tense, and his leg suddenly throbbed in protest. He had to struggle for the Jedi calm that was necessary before battle. He and Qui-Gon did not usually argue. Since their rupture when he had left the Jedi order, they had learned to honor each other's moods and inclinations. Even when they disagreed, they had found harmony. One of them stepped back and let the other make the decision. Usually it was Obi-Wan who let Qui-Gon lead, as a Padawan should. But as he grew older, his Master often let Obi-Wan choose, just as he had allowed Obi-Wan to choose a path back on Ragoon-6 during their tracking exercise. They never separated in anger after a disagreement.

Obi-Wan was startled at how disappointed and angry he still felt about Qui-Gon's decision. The wind was cooling his hot cheeks, but not his disquiet.

Would this disagreement shake their union? He didn't know. He had felt distance between them since they arrived on New Apsolon. Perhaps this would deepen it.

He couldn't worry about it. He had spoken the truth. But the distance he felt from his Master saddened him.

Obi-Wan turned his mind away from the disagreement and used the time to focus. He would need a sure connection to the Force. His wound would slow him down somewhat, and Qui-Gon would not be there to cover him. He would have to rely on strategy more than speed.

They were approaching the Rock Worker settlement when Yanci signaled them. She turned the swoop away and led them toward a split in a sheer wall. Eritha's landspeeder cleared the opening with just centimeters to spare.

"They won't find her here," Yanci said. "I doubt they'd be looking for strays. We think their object was to steal our most advanced explosives."

"I will contact you when the situation is safe," Obi-Wan told Eritha.

She looked reluctant, but she nodded.

Suddenly, he felt a surge in the Force. He whipped his head around and saw nothing.

Yanci zoomed out of the crack in the canyon wall, and he followed. He quickly scanned the horizon and saw Qui-Gon's landspeeder in the distance, gaining fast.

Obi-Wan signaled to Yanci, then headed out to meet Qui-Gon. When he caught up to the landspeeder, he hovered by Qui-Gon's side.

Qui-Gon looked at him directly. His face showed the signs of a great internal struggle. "I was wrong, Padawan. Thank you for pointing it out to me. My duty lies here. No matter," he said with difficulty, "what it may cost."

Obi-Wan nodded. "I'm glad you came back."

Gunning their motors, they caught up to Yanci.

"I'm taking you around a back way," she told them. "When I left, we had managed to hold our position surrounding the unit where we keep the supplies and explosives."

They didn't need the caution. They took a roundabout way, skirting the settlement. Yanci slowed her speeder as they approached a road cut through a narrow canyon.

Obi-Wan listened for the sounds of battle, but heard nothing except the wind. The quiet was eerie. He glanced over at Qui-Gon and saw his Master frown.

Something lay in the road ahead. Obi-Wan didn't need to come closer to know what it was. The deep disturbance in the Force told him everything.

Yanci slowed to a crawl, almost stalling her swoop. "It's a body," she said shakily.

Suddenly, she gunned the engine and zoomed ahead. Obi-Wan and Qui-Gon speeded up to catch her.

Yanci was off her swoop before it had stopped. It kept going and crashed, but she didn't react. She raced toward the body in the road. Her cry was terrible.

"Kevta!" She bent over the body. With tears streaming down her face, she checked for his vital signs. She placed her hands on his chest. "Kevta!" Her cry turned to a moan, and she collapsed, cradling his head.

Qui-Gon's face went pale. Obi-Wan saw that his Master could not tear his gaze away from the sight.

"Master," he said. "We need to go on, find out what happened . . ."

Qui-Gon's nod seemed to take forever. "One moment." His voice was hoarse.

He got off the landspeeder and walked to Yanci's side. He crouched by her and put a hand on her shoulder. He did not speak a word. He let his presence balance her grief until she was able to lift her head.

"I left him," she said, her voice broken. "He made me go. I am the best on a swoop, he said. I am the one who knows the quarries best. I was the one who could catch the Jedi. I left him!"

"You left in order to save your people," Qui-Gon said.

"And I failed them. If Kevta is dead, I don't want to see the rest of the camp." Yanci gently laid her head on Kevta's chest. "I will stay here. I can't leave him."

Qui-Gon squeezed her shoulder. Then he stood. Wordlessly, he nodded at Obi-Wan. The two Jedi knew what they were about to find. Death lay ahead of them.

They walked farther into the camp. Some of the dwellings were still smoking from fires the Absolutes had set. Bodies lay alongside the road. The Rock Workers still clutched the tools they had used as weapons.

Obi-Wan saw Bini on the ground. Her sightless eyes stared up at the sky. He knelt beside her and gently closed her eyelids. "Sleep well," he murmured.

Qui-Gon entered the school. Several long moments passed before he exited. "It is better for you not to go in," he told Obi-Wan. "The Rock Workers tried to hide the children there. The Absolutes left no one alive."

Obi-Wan turned away. Qui-Gon was right. He did not need to see it.

The sound of a speeder rose above the eerie quiet. Eritha rode slowly toward them, her head turning to take in the devastation. She stopped the speeder and got out shakily.

"This is what they are capable of," she said, her face ashen. "I didn't know. Alani can't be part of this. She must not know the things that they are willing to do."

They continued their grim tour, looking for survivors. The death toll was complete. There was not a living being in the camp.

As they started back, they saw Yanci walking

toward them. Her legs moved, but she did not seem to be powering them herself. She moved like a droid, with jerky, articulated motion.

"Everyone is gone," she said. "It was a massacre. There is nothing I can do. I can't find Bini —"

"I'm sorry," Obi-Wan said gently. "I found her."

Yanci bowed her head. "I was jealous of Bini. She was close to Kevta. It was stupid of me. I can never tell her that." She wandered away and sat on the ground, her head in her hands.

"Yanci," Qui-Gon called. "Can you tell us what the Absolutes took this time?"

She lifted her head. "Everything," she said numbly. "All our blasting equipment is gone."

Qui-Gon nodded. It was what he had expected. "Let's look for clues," he said in a low tone to Obi-Wan.

They started with the target of the Absolutes — the sheds where the blasting equipment was stored. Here the fiercest fighting had taken place. Obi-Wan pushed down the revulsion he felt rise in his throat at the desperate postures of the dead. They lay as they had died, fighting to the last.

He concentrated on the task, picking over the ground carefully, then moving into the shed.

Qui-Gon stooped and sifted something through his fingers. When he held up his hand to Obi-Wan, his fingers were stained red.

"This soil is not from this area," he said. "The Absolutes tracked it in. Look at the boot marks. They aren't the same patterns as the Rock Workers'."

Obi-Wan bent and took a small sample of soil. He tapped it into a specimen container from his utility belt. "Let's ask Yanci. She said she knew the quarries better than anyone."

They returned to Yanci, and Obi-Wan showed her the soil. She rubbed it between her fingers.

"Red," she murmured. "I've seen this soil." She closed her eyes. When she opened them, her gaze was filled with certainty. "I know exactly where their hideout is."

CHAPTER 13

Within minutes, Qui-Gon, Obi-Wan, and Eritha were back on their transports. They had entered the coordinates Yanci had come up with into their nav systems.

Qui-Gon turned to Eritha. "I cannot order you to stay here. But I strongly recommend that you do so."

She shook her head. "You haven't been able to get rid of me yet. After seeing this, how can I stay behind?"

Qui-Gon turned away, displeased. It would be so much easier if he did not have to worry about Eritha. Despite her strong words, he knew she was not prepared for what they might find.

"The site is to the west, in the quarries abandoned years ago. As you get closer, the canyons will narrow," Yanci warned. "You will have to abandon your vehicles, even the swoop. You must approach on foot. There is a road, but I'm sure it will be under surveillance. This is the best way to approach without being seen."

"What will you do?" Obi-Wan asked, concerned. The haunted look had not left Yanci's eyes. She had been damaged and would never be the same.

"I will bury my dead," Yanci said.

"I contacted the Workers in the city," Eritha told her. "They are sending help to you. They will be here by dawn tomorrow. Will you be all right?"

"I am with those I love," Yanci said. "I wish you success on your mission."

Qui-Gon turned away. He felt a heaviness inside him. For the first time since he had become a Jedi Knight, he could not face someone's grief. Grief was part of life, and Jedi saw it more than most. Qui-Gon knew the forms it could take, how it could twist and spiral into rage or revenge or dead numbness. There had been times when sorrow had been so much a part of what he saw that it became the only thing he saw. Part of his training had been to see the joy in the galaxy that existed alongside the grief. He remembered early in his life as a Jedi Knight how he had returned to the Temple for long talks with Yoda. Yoda had helped him see the balance in the galaxy, just as he had taught him the balance in the Force.

But now he looked at Yanci, and he saw a possibility of what he would become. His eyes would be that empty. His heart would be that shattered.

Qui-Gon accelerated the engines. The wind blew in his face, making his eyes tear. He knew he was pushing his craft in order to outrun his fear, and he knew it was not what a Jedi should do. But at that moment, the wind and the speed comforted him as no Jedi wisdom could.

Now that they had a clear direction, they made good time through the quarries. The landscape was rough, with unexpected looming cliffs and canyons. Yanci had prepared them for switchbacks and sudden huge pits of water as large as lakes.

At last they reached an area where the canyons narrowed to mere slits in the cliff walls. They abandoned their transports as Yanci had told them. They proceeded single file through the narrow passages.

Qui-Gon took the lead. Ahead he saw a line of sky and ground and knew that soon they would be through. He slowed his pace and drew up to the opening.

In front of him the cliffs widened to embrace

a small canyon. A deep pit was to the right, filled with water. The soil around the pit was a muddy red dotted with huge boulders. Sunlight danced on the smooth surface of the water. Some distance to the left he could see the dark opening of a cave. He saw no movement, no sign of living beings.

Obi-Wan and Eritha crowded behind him to scrutinize the area.

"There's no one here," Eritha said, disappointed. "Yanci was wrong."

Obi-Wan spoke quietly. "What do you think, Master? Are we in the wrong place?"

Qui-Gon reached out for the Force. He tested the air, searching for vibrations. He sent a message to Tahl. *I am here.*

He received something back — a reverberation. Like a gentle touch on his cheek. Like a tiny sigh. Something . . .

"No," he said. "This is the place."

Suddenly they saw the water ripple on the lake. The ripples grew into waves. The two Jedi grew alert.

"We're wasting time. We should go back," Eritha said.

The two Jedi remained focused on the lake. "There is no wind," Obi-Wan said.

"Exactly," Qui-Gon murmured.

A structure rose from the surface. Water

streamed off its curved top. An opening slowly widened and a ramp emerged. It extended over the water to dry land. A few seconds later, two tech vehicles sped down the ramp, hit land, and then headed for the cave. They disappeared inside. They did not see the Jedi.

"Everything is hidden," Qui-Gon said. "The camp can't be seen from the air. Clever."

"How shall we infiltrate, then?" Obi-Wan asked.

"We'll have to start with the cave. The tech vehicles didn't seem to go through a checkpoint," Qui-Gon said, scanning the cave entrance. "I don't think there are sensors outside the cave." He turned back to Eritha. "Stay here until we send for you."

"No. If you go without me, I'll follow you." Eritha's jaw set.

Qui-Gon frowned. "Then stay behind us. Realize that you can endanger this mission if you act hastily. You will follow my orders. Agreed?"

"Agreed." Eritha flashed a shaky grin. "I'm stubborn, but I'm not stupid."

"All right," Qui-Gon muttered. "Let's go."

CHAPTER 14

They kept close to the cliff walls and boulders for as long as they could. Then they purposefully walked the short distance to the cave entrance. Qui-Gon and Obi-Wan checked for scanners as they moved closer but saw none. Obi-Wan guessed that the Absolutes considered their hideout so well hidden that they did not need to install them.

They slipped into the darkness of the cave entrance with relief. Immediately to the right was a pen where gravsleds and small speeders were kept. There was a bin filled with tech jackets. Qui-Gon signaled to the others, and they each donned one. Eritha hid her hair under a cap and dirtied her face, so she was less recognizable.

Feeling a little less exposed, they proceeded farther into the cave. Glow rods set high in the walls gave faint illumination. They could see that the small opening to the cave was deceptive. As they moved deeper into it, the space widened and extended far in the distance.

"It goes out under the water," Qui-Gon said in a low tone. "This is bigger than it appears."

Ahead a few Absolutes in the same tech jackets came walking toward them. Qui-Gon gave them an impersonal nod of greeting. They nodded back and continued walking.

Eritha let out a shaky breath. "Whew."

"It appears that there are enough Absolutes working here that not everyone knows one another," Qui-Gon murmured. "Good. Obi-Wan, look for any high-security devices on the tunnels leading off the cave. That could mean that Tahl is being held there."

Obi-Wan could feel his Master's tension. They were so close now. He reached out to the Force to help him with his perceptions. Nothing could go wrong now. If they were captured, it would mean a delay that could cost Tahl her life.

They paused by a tunnel that was lined with computer equipment. "This must be the tech-control area," Qui-Gon said. He moved away quickly as someone walked out of a durasteel door and began checking the equipment.

They walked on, passing other beings who either nodded or walked quickly, focused on their business. Eritha kept her face turned away in case she was recognized despite her disguise. Obi-Wan noted a security sensor bank near an offshoot tunnel. He pointed it out to Qui-Gon.

"Let's try it," Qui-Gon said.

Obi-Wan studied the offshoot tunnel entrance. "There's a retinal scan grid to the right. If we pass through, an alarm will go off."

Qui-Gon studied the sensors and the retinal scan carefully. "They mounted it too low," he said. "I think if we use cable launchers, we can swing over the sensors without tripping them. They probably didn't have time to perfect the system. Look at the drill marks around the sensors. This was done recently."

"Since Balog brought Tahl here?" Obi-Wan asked.

"Maybe." Qui-Gon turned to Eritha. "You must stay here, Eritha. Alert us with the silent alarm on your comlink if there's trouble. We'll be back as soon as we can. If a patrol comes, walk away as though you have a destination, then circle back. If you hear an alarm sound, hide. It does not necessarily mean that Obi-Wan and I have been captured. Turn on your homing device on your comlink and we'll find you."

Eritha nodded. "I'll be all right."

Obi-Wan saw that Qui-Gon didn't like to leave her, but they had no choice. He watched as his Master aimed carefully, sending his cable launcher high into the air to bite into the ceiling of the offshoot tunnel. He activated the launcher and it carried him high above. His head almost bumped the ceiling of the cave, but he cleared the sensors and landed on the other side.

Obi-Wan hoped he would have the same graceful skill. He followed Qui-Gon's lead, holding his breath until his own cable launcher was secure. Then he activated the launch mode. It pulled him up quickly, and he scraped against the rough ceiling. He was over the range of the sensors, and was pulled into the tunnel. He landed next to Qui-Gon.

They hurried down the tunnel. At the end was a durasteel door set into the cave wall. There was no security panel outside the door.

"What now? If Tahl is in there, someone could be with her."

Qui-Gon closed his eyes. "I don't feel her," he said in a low voice. "But we need to find out why this tunnel has such high security when the others don't. We have to go in."

He activated his lightsaber and cut through the durasteel, making an opening big enough for them to walk through. Qui-Gon ducked inside the room, and Obi-Wan quickly followed.

They were in a storage area filled with bins and crates. There was no sign of Tahl or of the sensory deprivation device she had been imprisoned in. Instead, the room was filled with explosives. Crate after crate was labeled, showing that there were extremely powerful devices within.

"This must be what they stole from the Rock Workers," Obi-Wan said.

"And some bought on the black market, as well," Qui-Gon added. "Look. This is Mota's mark. They have enough explosives here to level the city."

Obi-Wan looked worriedly at his Master. "What does this mean?"

"That they are prepared to take over with violence, if they must," Qui-Gon said. "But why the change in plan? As far as we knew, the Absolutes were working to gain power through infiltration and deceit."

Qui-Gon gave a last swift look around. "Let's go, Padawan. There's nothing here to lead us to Tahl. And I don't like leaving Eritha back there alone."

Not to mention that they had left a gaping hole in a security door, Obi-Wan thought. As soon as that was discovered, the complex would go on alert.

They ran back down the tunnel toward the main cave. Suddenly, Obi-Wan felt a disturbance in the Force. His steps slowed just as Qui-Gon's did.

They didn't need to compare notes. They both knew what they had felt. Something had gone wrong.

They melted back against the wall of the tunnel, then proceeded carefully. The cave came into sight. They saw Eritha surrounded by security. Obviously she was trying to bluff, and not succeeding. She gave one last, desperate look down the tunnel.

Qui-Gon put his hand on Obi-Wan's arm to prevent him from moving.

"We can't," he murmured. "As soon as they see us, they'll sound an alarm. Whoever is holding Tahl will know the cave has been invaded. We can't risk it. Let's see how Eritha deals with this."

Eritha pitched her voice loudly, and it echoed off the walls of the cave. "You fools, don't you know who I am? I am Eritha, daughter of Ewane. Contact my sister Alani right this minute. We are *helping* the Absolutes, you idiots!"

"You are a Worker —" one of the security officers started.

"I am a patriot!" Eritha shouted. "Now let me go!"

"We'll have to check this out first," the officer said. "You'll have to come with us."

"I will not forget this!" Eritha said as they placed her in the center of the group and began to march her off. "I will get each of your names and you will be hearing from us!"

"She certainly didn't show fear," Obi-Wan said admiringly.

"Yes, she handled it well," Qui-Gon said as he stepped out from the shelter of the tunnel wall. "Unfortunately, now we have two to rescue."

CHAPTER 15

Qui-Gon and Obi-Wan waited a moment, then slipped out of the tunnel. Obi-Wan could see that his Master was disturbed by this turn of events. They kept a good distance between themselves and Eritha and her guards, but kept her in sight. The guards marched her farther inside the cave until they came to another high-security entrance to a tunnel. One of the guards accessed the security panel and punched in a code, then pressed his eye against the sensor. When the sensor cleared him, they half-carried Eritha through the opening and down the tunnel.

"They could be keeping Tahl there," Obi-Wan said. "No doubt it's where they take prisoners."

"Most likely," Qui-Gon said. He studied the tunnel entrance. "But this time we are not so lucky. The sensors are well placed. We won't be able to get in without attracting attention. When those sensors go off, we could be putting Eritha's and Tahl's lives in danger. And the Absolutes aren't stupid. They probably suspect that Eritha wasn't alone when she infiltrated the cave."

"Any other ideas?"

"I think there's only one thing to do," Qui-Gon said. "We need a diversion."

They retraced their steps back to the weapons tunnel. Using the same method, they propelled themselves past the sensors and safely into the tunnel. Then they ran back to the room where the explosives were kept.

Qui-Gon quickly read the labels on the various bins. "We must be careful," he warned. "Too much, and we risk collapsing the cave. But there has to be enough to cause confusion and chaos."

Obi-Wan was not an expert on explosives. He let Qui-Gon choose what they needed. Qui-Gon handed him a supply of small explosives.

"We'll have to set these up away from here," Qui-Gon said. "If we're too close, it could cause a chain reaction."

He tucked more explosives inside his tunic along with timing devices. "This should do it. No one should get hurt, but there will be confusion. That's all we'll need. As soon as we get Tahl and Eritha, we'll head to the cave entrance."

"What if we're spotted?" Obi-Wan asked. "No doubt everyone will be heading there."

"We'll have to get a tech jacket for Tahl. We'll just have to count on the smoke and confusion."

Obi-Wan remembered what Lenz and Irini had said about the drug that was used to paralyze subjects inside the deprivation device. He was prepared for the fact that Tahl might not be able to walk or move. Qui-Gon did not seem to want to deal with that possibility.

"Hurry, Obi-Wan. We need to get to Eritha before they do something to her."

Obi-Wan followed Qui-Gon back to the cave. They set a small amount of explosives farther down the cave, toward the entrance, then a second at the entrance to the tech-control tunnel. Then they hurried back toward the transport pen.

"We'll set these to go off later," Qui-Gon said. "It will be a small explosion, but it should destroy most of the transports. Just in case we're followed." He grabbed another tech jacket and rolled it up, shoving it inside his own. "Now let's get back to where they took Eritha."

Obi-Wan had seen his Master focused before. This was different. His gaze was intent, his every movement economical. Although Obi-Wan could feel Qui-Gon's anxiety, there was no trace of it in his speech or his actions. He appeared completely calm. Where did the desperation go? Obi-Wan admired how his Master had taken his emotion and given it discipline and purpose. It was a supreme example of how a Jedi should act.

They were steps away from the first tunnel offshoot when the initial explosion went off. The cave seemed to rock for a moment, the walls and rocks shuddering. A siren wailed, and suddenly Absolutes appeared in the cave halls, running out from the various branches and tunnels.

"It's back that way!" Qui-Gon shouted. He feinted a move in that direction and he and Obi-Wan ran a few steps. They let themselves be overtaken before turning back the way they were headed.

Smoke began to drift back toward them. Obi-Wan saw a figure appear and disappear ahead of them amid the drifting smoke.

"I think it's Balog," he said to Qui-Gon. "He's headed toward the explosives tunnel."

They melted back against the cave wall and watched as Balog went through the retinal scan and hurried back toward the tunnel.

"Should we follow?" Obi-Wan asked.

"Let's wait here. We know Tahl isn't back there. When he returns, we'll follow him," Qui-Gon said.

Another explosion split the air. Smoke rolled back toward them.

"That should be the tech center," Qui-Gon said.

Suddenly Balog appeared, darting out of the side tunnel. Obi-Wan recognized his squat, muscular body and powerful stride. Ignoring those who were rushing toward the cave entrance, he headed in the opposite direction.

Qui-Gon nodded grimly. "When one's home is burning, one goes for the most valuable item."

"He's heading for Tahl," Obi-Wan agreed.

The two Jedi followed him. Obi-Wan expected Balog to turn toward the tunnel where Eritha was being held, but he kept going. Another explosion rocked the cave. This time it was followed by another, smaller boom.

"The fuel tanks of the vehicles," Qui-Gon said.

They passed a side tunnel with a readout sign: UW BASE ENTRANCE. Obi-Wan took note of it as he passed. It had to be the entrance to the underwater part of the secret complex.

Balog abruptly turned into a small tunnel without security sensors. They plunged into the tunnel behind him. The glow rods were not operational, and the darkness was almost complete. They could only see the gleam of a dura-steel door just ahead.

Balog paused outside the door to access it. Obi-Wan hesitated, unsure of what to do. But beside him, Qui-Gon was already moving. His Master put on a burst of speed as Balog slipped through the door. With a mighty leap, Qui-Gon followed him, and the door slid shut.

CHAPTER 16

Qui-Gon landed with his lightsaber already activated. Behind him, he heard the door close.

Balog stood in the center of the room between Qui-Gon and Tahl. The sensory deprivation device was leaning against the cave wall with Tahl inside. He could only see her eyes through a small viewscreen. He knew she was alive. Her eyelids fluttered. She could still feel his presence, as she always had. A slight tremor in the Force told him that she was trying to reach out to him.

Obi-Wan began to cut through the durasteel with his lightsaber. Qui-Gon could smell the melting metal. He kept his gaze steady on Balog, who was smiling faintly.

Then Balog laughed.

"You think you can threaten me? You think that you and your young friend can frighten me? What you don't know is that I have all the power here." He held up a small transmitter. "I can take away her life."

Obi-Wan burst through the hole in the door and stopped short, his lightsaber ready.

"Don't move, Obi-Wan," Qui-Gon said steadily.

"Do you see this?" Balog asked, holding the transmitter aloft. "I can give your friend a last, lethal dose. She is very weak. I wanted to keep her alive, but I've come to realize that there is no need."

"What do you want?" Qui-Gon asked.

"Nothing from you," Balog said contemptuously. "You've done enough already. You found this place. Well, your Worker allies won't find anything here when they arrive. No records. Nothing to spy on, nothing to steal."

"You set the weapons room to detonate," Qui-Gon guessed.

"I'll be gone before that happens. We have plenty of support in the city. We don't need these followers to accomplish what we need to."

"You don't care what lives are lost."

"I care about Apsolon. *My* Apsolon," Balog said fiercely. "Not the Apsolon the Workers want. You Jedi are in my way." He stepped back and accessed a door behind him. A tiny space contained a small transport with a bubble-shaped top. Another door was cut into the far wall. No doubt it was to allow the exit of the transport into the lake. The interior door would close, allowing the compartment to flood.

"Now I'm leaving. You may make it out of here when the explosives room goes, but I doubt it — especially when you have to drag your friend along." Balog pointed to Tahl with his chin. "And believe me, she's in no shape to walk. I made sure of that."

Qui-Gon tensed, then relaxed. It took an effort of will to absorb his anger and continue to wait for his opening.

"I leave you to your fate," Balog said, stepping back toward the transport. His small, dark eyes glinted. "Don't move, either of you. You see my finger near this button? If you try to stop me and are a fraction off, if you stumble, if you give me only a split second, I can press it. If you move toward me, I could flinch and press it. If, in short, one of the thousand things that could go wrong does go wrong, Tahl will die."

Qui-Gon sprang. He had never moved faster or more surely. He knew that Balog did not see him, that one moment he was standing meters away and the next he was in the air next to him. With careful precision, Qui-Gon brought his lightsaber down, neatly slicing off Balog's finger. The transmitter fell to the floor.

"I guess you didn't flinch," Qui-Gon said.

Howling with pain and rage, Balog backed up

toward the transport as he fumbled for his blaster with his good hand. Obi-Wan sprang forward as Qui-Gon headed for Tahl. Another explosion rocked the cave, this one larger than before. The force of the blast almost knocked Obi-Wan to the ground. The sensory deprivation device began to slide. Qui-Gon threw himself toward it and caught it in his arms. He laid it down gently.

Instead of attacking Obi-Wan, Balog aimed his fire at the sensory deprivation device. Qui-Gon ignored the ping of blaster fire around his head; he knew his Padawan would deflect it. A chain of explosions went off and dirt began to rain down from the cave ceiling. Obi-Wan sprang into the tiny holding room as Balog scrambled into the transport.

"Leave him, Obi-Wan!" Qui-Gon shouted. He put his lightsaber to work, cutting away at the deprivation device.

Balog accessed the exit. Water poured into the tiny room, knocking Obi-Wan off his feet. His lightsaber shorted out.

Qui-Gon had a bigger worry: Soon the room would be flooded.

"Obi-Wan!"

Balog's transport took off underwater, bouncing wildly as it fought against the impact of the water gushing toward the opening.

"Let him go!" Qui-Gon bellowed. "Tahl will

drown!" The deprivation device was now floating. Qui-Gon held his lightsaber aloft. If it touched the water, it would short out, too. Qui-Gon could feel Tahl's life force flickering. They had to get her out of here.

Obi-Wan struggled to his feet. The water was now up to his knees. He felt his leg ache as he pushed toward Qui-Gon, who had opened a seam in the side of the device.

"That sounded like the main weapons room," Qui-Gon said tersely. "The cave could collapse. Let's get Tahl out of here."

Water was now almost to their waists. Qui-Gon deactivated his lightsaber and quickly tucked it into his belt. Desperately, he lifted Tahl out of the device. She said nothing, her head flopping against his chest as though she couldn't support it. To see her so weak sent agony ripping through him. They struggled through the water toward the opening Obi-Wan had cut in the door.

Once they were through the opening, they were able to stand. Water was pouring through the opening, and the door was starting to strain against its bolts, but the water in the tunnel was only ankle deep. They ran, splashing through the flooding, and reached the dry area of the cave. The smoke was thick and acrid now, burning their lungs. The cave area was deserted.

Qui-Gon allowed Tahl to slide down his body so that she was on her feet. Her legs immediately gave way. He picked her up again and cradled her against him. He had to control his anger against Balog for her sake. What she needed from him was calm.

"Tahl," he said gently. "We're going to get you out of here."

One hand curled around his neck. He felt the gesture, her cold hand against his neck, and it curdled his blood. It was the same gesture she had made in the vision, the gesture that had told him how close to death she was.

She managed to smile up at him. "It is too late for me, dear friend," she said softly.

CHAPTER 17

They knew the Jedi Masters were watching. They were only ten years old, too young yet to be chosen as Padawans. But they knew the choice was coming soon. Some Jedi students had been chosen as young as eleven.

It was called Exhibition Day, and they had performed exercises while the Jedi Masters watched. Force exercises, balance, endurance, climbing, jumping, swimming. Sometimes they split into teams of two or four. It was play, but it was also serious.

The last exercise was a series of training lightsaber matches. Some were done blindfolded. Some pitted one student against two attackers. Qui-Gon won all his matches. It came down to him and Clee Rhara and Tahl. Then Tahl beat Clee Rhara.

"Guess that leaves us," she whispered as she bowed to him at the start of the final match. "Don't worry. I'll go easy on you."

They had been matched many times before. He knew how fast she was. She knew how strong he was. Knowing each other's strengths made the match more interesting. Qui-Gon found fighting Tahl to be both exhausting and exhilarating. It brought out his best skills.

They whirled around the space, using every inch of wall and floor. All the Jedi students admired Tahl's gymnastic abilities. She could run up a wall, twist, and come at you with a sweeping backhand twist that left you dizzy.

Tahl fought hard. Qui-Gon admired how just when he thought she was tiring, she would find fresh strength. He could not match her agility, but he was able to surprise her with strategy. He saw her eyes flash with astonishment and her teeth grit in determination as she parried his blows and came at him with a series of twists and reversals.

The match was not timed. It would only end when one of them scored a blow. Exhaustion began to slow their moves, but they did not stop or make mistakes. He could hear the murmur among the spectators, wondering how long the two students could continue. He sensed more Jedi Masters arriving.

Tahl's face was a mask. She had gone deep within herself, past her exhaustion to a place of sheer will. Qui-Gon had never felt so tired. His arm muscles shook. His legs felt watery. They trembled. Still he did not stop or make a mistake.

Then Tahl's foot slipped. Just a fraction, but it was enough. The floor was wet with their sweat. She left herself vulnerable for one split second, and he moved forward, kicking out with one foot and driving the lightsaber from her grasp. At the same time he brought his own lightsaber close to her. He did not touch her with it. He was not willing to give her even the slightest sting from the training saber.

"Match to Qui-Gon," one of the Jedi Masters spoke.

Qui-Gon and Tahl bowed to each other. Then they collapsed together on a bench nearby.

"A good match," he said, panting.

"It would have been better if I'd won."

He shook his head. "Don't you ever give up?"

She wiped the sweat off her forehead with a towel. "Never."

Qui-Gon felt disoriented, as though he were in a dream. He was living inside his vision. His greatest fear had visited him. He thought he had known desperation in that vision, but the living reality was far worse.

Tahl's eyes closed, and she slumped against him. He felt her muscles go slack, and she melted against him as though she no longer had bones. He had never realized Tahl could feel so soft against him. He had only known her strength. He held her against his chest.

"You should leave me," she whispered. "I don't have long . . ."

He leaned his head down to speak into her ear. "No. It is not too late. You never give up. The Force is still with you. I am with you. You cannot leave me now. Not now."

"I . . . will try, for you," she breathed.

"Qui-Gon, we must go," Obi-Wan said desperately.

He nodded and let his Padawan lead the way. Tahl was no burden. She felt light in his arms.

Fissures had opened in the ceiling, and water streamed in from above. The cave was slowly collapsing. Water poured out of the side tunnel where Balog had left.

"Do you think we can reach the cave entrance?" Obi-Wan asked.

Qui-Gon eyed the water pouring from the ceiling and the thick smoke ahead. "Doubtful. We can try to find another way out."

"There is another . . . exit," Tahl said. Qui-Gon had to bend down to hear her. "To the underwater base."

"I saw it," Obi-Wan said. "Let's try it. But what about Eritha?"

Qui-Gon hesitated. "Let's get to the entrance to the underwater base first." He did not want to have to decide between Tahl's life and Eritha's. But he knew he could not leave without looking for the young girl.

Tahl stirred again. "Eritha is here? We can't leave her, we must . . ." Each word seemed to cost her a great effort.

Qui-Gon stilled her with a hand on her hair. "We won't."

The cave had been evacuated. Another explosion shook the cave and they staggered with its power. More water streamed from the ceiling.

They reached the side tunnel that led to the underwater structure. Obi-Wan looked at Qui-Gon anxiously as the water grew deeper, now swirling around their knees. It was icy cold.

"The tunnel where Eritha was held is just ahead," Qui-Gon said. "Try there first. I will stay here with Tahl. If Eritha is not there, come back here." If necessary, he would get Tahl out and return for Eritha. He could feel how weak Tahl's connection to the Force was. It frightened him.

Obi-Wan turned to hurry away, but from the smoky dimness they suddenly saw a figure pushing through the water toward them. It was Eritha, her braided hair now loose and wet.

"They left me! They forgot about me!" she screamed, almost collapsing in Obi-Wan's arms. "They set off explosives. The cave is collapsing!"

"It's all right," Obi-Wan told her. "We'll get you out of here."

He supported her and brought her back to Qui-Gon. Qui-Gon accessed the entrance to the underwater structure. They squeezed through quickly to prevent more water from flooding the connecting tunnel.

The relative dryness of the connecting tunnel was reassuring. Smoke had not penetrated, and they breathed easier. The Absolutes had not chosen to blow up the underwater structure . . . yet.

The connecting tunnel was fabricated from white duraplast, with occasional transparent viewscreens that allowed watery light to filter in from above. They passed through it quickly and entered the main structure.

This was obviously where the majority of the tech centers were housed. The cave had been used for storage. They passed room after room of holofile cabinets and computer banks. The offices were empty. No doubt this part of the complex had been evacuated as well.

"Do you think Balog is planning to blow this area, too?" Obi-Wan asked Qui-Gon.

"Possibly. But he might not have had time. We need to find the ramp that can get us to shore." Qui-Gon knew the shore of the lake was to his right. As soon as they found a main corridor, it would lead to the ramp exit.

Obi-Wan ran ahead with Eritha. When they came to a main corridor, Qui-Gon was glad to see his Padawan turn right. He relaxed a bit, allowing his Padawan to lead them. He turned his attention to Tahl.

He could see a pale blue vein throb near one of her closed eyes. It reassured him. Her life systems were still operating, her body still functioning. The weakness he felt could be reversed. Her systems had been shut down for several days. It would take time for her to regain her strength. That was all she needed. Time. He held her more securely against him.

Ahead, he saw Obi-Wan stop at the ramp control. He pressed his eye against the panel.

"There's an electroscope," he said, drawing

away as Qui-Gon came up. "I don't think we can activate the ramp. We'd be spotted easily."

Qui-Gon leaned forward and put his eye against the electroscope. It gave a view of the shore and the cave entrance. Smoke continued to billow out from the cave. Absolutes gathered on the shore. Someone was organizing a retreat with the remaining functioning vehicles. If they activated the ramp, they would land right in the middle of them. Obi-Wan was right. Qui-Gon felt sure that even if the Jedi weren't recognized, Eritha or Tahl would be. Eritha had lost her tech jacket. Tahl was in no condition to walk.

"We have to swim," Qui-Gon decided. "If we swim far enough away, we can skirt those boulders and pass through the canyon to our vehicles." He hesitated. "Can you?" he asked Obi-Wan. "Your leg . . ."

"I can," Obi-Wan said firmly. "I'll give my breather to Eritha."

Qui-Gon lowered Tahl carefully to the floor. Her feet couldn't hold her, so he laid her gently down. He took out his breather from his utility belt.

"Tahl?"

Her head turned. Qui-Gon's heart broke at how lackluster her response was.

"We have to swim. Can you use a breather?"

There was a quirk at the edge of her lips. Almost a smile. "Only since I was three."

He smiled and gently fitted the tube on her. "When we get to the beach, we'll have a short way to walk. I'll carry you. Our transports aren't far."

She nodded slightly. He knew she was saving her strength.

Qui-Gon motioned to the emergency exit lever. Eritha had donned Obi-Wan's breather. Qui-Gon knew that it would be a long swim for Obi-Wan. Obi-Wan was a powerful swimmer, but the leg injury worried Qui-Gon.

They accessed the door, which opened into a small chamber. There was a panel in the ceiling. Slowly, the chamber began to fill with water. The water was cold, and Qui-Gon felt Tahl's involuntary shiver. They floated up toward the ceiling. Qui-Gon nodded at Obi-Wan and the two Jedi took their deepest breath. The panel slid open and they swam out.

Qui-Gon did not feel the cold water. He did not feel fatigued. Tahl felt buoyant in his arms, so buoyant that he felt his hopes rise. He swam with his Padawan by his side. Both of them kept their eye on Eritha, with Obi-Wan drifting back to help her if she lagged.

His lungs began to ache. The smoke had weakened them. Qui-Gon peered ahead, but couldn't see the shoreline. There would be no gradual rise, since the pit was dug for mining purposes. His speed was hampered by being able to use only one arm, but his kicks were powerful and propelled him forward.

At last Obi-Wan's feet touched bottom. He surfaced, then quickly signaled an okay. Qui-Gon surfaced as well, taking deep lungfuls of air. Obi-Wan was doing the same.

Even as they took deep breaths, they moved toward the shore. The Absolutes were lining up to be transported away. No one noticed them as they ran up the short distance to the boulders. From there it was easy to slip into the narrow crevices between the high cliffs. The rough ground made for hard walking. Qui-Gon's arms began to ache with the effort of holding Tahl. Obi-Wan was limping slightly, but he still was able to move quickly.

"Almost there," Qui-Gon told Tahl. He did not know if she was conscious.

They found their transports where they had left them. Relief flooded Qui-Gon. His last fear was that the Absolutes would have found them.

"Take my landspeeder, Qui-Gon," Eritha offered. "It is faster than yours."

"Thank you." Qui-Gon gently placed Tahl in the companion seat.

He swung into the pilot seat and glanced over.

As always, she could sense when he was looking at her. And as always, she could sense his mood.

"Stop being so worried," she said quietly.

"I'll try."

"I'm gaining strength every moment from your strength."

He took her hand. He called up the Force from the air around them. He felt her do the same, though her hold on the Force was weak. It was all right. He would provide the extra strength she needed. He felt their power combine.

Eritha came to stand by the speeder. "Go directly to the Supreme Governor's residence," she said. "I will call ahead and have med care waiting for you."

Qui-Gon nodded his thanks. He activated the engines.

"I will see you in New Apsolon," he told Obi-Wan. He reached inside his tunic and handed Tahl's lightsaber to Obi-Wan. "Until yours recharges."

"I will guard it with my life." Obi-Wan swallowed. The concern in his eyes was all for Tahl. He gently touched her shoulder. "Safe journey."

Tahl answered weakly. "Thank you for finding me, Obi-Wan."

"May the Force be with you," Obi-Wan said.

"It is," Qui-Gon said confidently, and raced off.

CHAPTER 18

There was still a long journey ahead of them to New Apsolon. Qui-Gon would not stop. He would drive through the rest of the day and the night. With the extra power of Eritha's landspeeder, he should be at the edge of New Apsolon by dawn.

Tahl slid into a deep sleep. That would restore her. Qui-Gon reached for a thermal cape and covered her. The temperature fell as the suns slid down in the sky, melting over the horizon in tones of blazing red and gold. The rocks and cliffs around him turned pink. For the first time in a long while, Qui-Gon noticed the beauty. It was because Tahl was next to him, and he wanted her to be a part of it. He did not wake her, but silently he told her, *Do not leave me. We have so much left to share together.*

The moons rose, three delicate, luminous

crescents. The stars seemed even more brilliant next to the waning moons. Qui-Gon activated the speeder's protective dome and turned on the heating unit. Whenever he reached over to check Tahl's pulse, the coldness of her skin shocked him. He did not feel hunger but he ate a food capsule and drank water. He had a long night to get through.

Hours later, Tahl awoke. She pulled herself up a little straighter. She looked more alert, Qui-Gon noted with relief.

"It's cold," she said.

Qui-Gon had felt too warm, but he set the heating unit to maximum. "It's the middle of the night."

"Thank you for everything you have done," Tahl said. "I don't like being rescued. I was furious at myself for being in that position again."

"Don't worry," Qui-Gon said. "You have rescued me in the past. I'm sure you will again."

"Balog wanted something from me. That's why he kept me alive."

"Don't talk now. Save your strength. There will be time in New Apsolon," Qui-Gon said.

"No, I need to tell you. There is a list of informers among the Workers —"

"I know this."

"Balog thought I had it. Naturally I pretended

I knew where it was. So he kept me alive. But in that deprivation device I had time to think. Why did he believe I had the list?"

"Because you were undercover and could have had access?" Qui-Gon suggested.

"Is that reason enough to kidnap me?" Tahl shook her head. "I don't think so. So I went over that last day undercover. I still don't know how they found out I was a Jedi."

"Perhaps it was Alani," Qui-Gon said. "Eritha claims that Alani is in league with Balog. She wants to take over as Supreme Governor."

"Alani?" Tahl asked, surprised. "But she found the way to smuggle me into the Absolutes in the first place."

"She had a reason to keep you there, perhaps," Qui-Gon said. "When you were no longer useful, she betrayed you."

"And perhaps she hoped I would find the list," Tahl said slowly. Every word was an effort. "Naturally I would tell the girls I had found it. I trusted them."

"Do you remember anything significant about your last day?"

The thermal cape slipped off her shoulders, and Tahl drew it around her. "So cold . . ." she murmured. "Someone helped me that last day. I had seconds to get out of the hideout before they came for me. I ran into a message runner named Oleg. He was a low-level member of the Absolutes. Instead of turning me in, he helped me. He showed me a door the message runners used. When I asked him why he helped me, he said he was escaping, too. He had been marked for interrogation by the Absolute leaders. He did not know why, but he was leaving before he could find out."

"Look," Qui-Gon said. "The lights of the city are ahead."

It was still dark. The city lights on the horizon seemed to merge with the stars.

"Almost there," Qui-Gon said. "Rest. We'll talk later."

Tahl's voice had been growing softer. Now she closed her eyes and slid into sleep.

Dawn grew slowly. The landscape lightened. The city grew closer. They were low on fuel, but the computer told him they would make it.

Tahl slept on as the suns broke free of the horizon. The orange rays lit her body, instantly transforming her skin into its usual radiant health. Qui-Gon knew it was an illusion, but he took comfort in the sight.

Qui-Gon quickly maneuvered the landspeeder through the crowded morning streets. He turned down State Boulevard toward the Supreme

Governor's residence. As he pulled up, a figure hurried down the steps toward them. It was Roan's brother, Manex.

"Eritha contacted me to say you were arriving," he said. "I have arranged the finest med care in the city for Tahl. It is a short distance away. If you'll follow me." Manex pointed to his own landspeeder.

Qui-Gon hesitated. It was odd that Manex had met them outside. Eritha had promised them access to her own med care, which was in the residence itself.

Manex took note of his hesitation. "You must trust me," he said urgently. "Did I not tell you that I have the best of everything? My med care is exceptional. The med squad once worked on victims of the Absolutes. They had the greatest success. The doctor knows Tahl's condition. He can help." Manex glanced at Tahl, whose head was back and her eyes were closed.

It was the compassionate, worried look in Manex's eyes more than his words that made Qui-Gon nod. His instincts told him that Manex was sincere. Tahl needed the best care.

"Good," Manex said at Qui-Gon's nod. He sprinted toward his landspeeder, moving quickly for a man of his bulk. He jumped in and took off.

Qui-Gon followed closely. Manex pulled up in front of a gray stone building a few blocks away.

Immediately the doors opened and a med team rushed out.

A doctor bent over Tahl. Her eyes fluttered open. He applied a diagnostic readout to the side of her neck and frowned at the results.

"Will she be all right?"

"We will do the best we can."

The med team transferred Tahl to a wheeled stretcher. She was gone before he had a chance to touch her hand or tell her he'd be waiting. Qui-Gon sat numbly in the pilot seat, the speeder controls solid in his clenched fists, willing his own control not to slip away.

CHAPTER 19

Qui-Gon sat by the shore of the lake and stared at the cliff. The rocky surface seemed completely sheer. The cliff looked impossibly big. But most things looked pretty big to him. He was eight years old.

They had already climbed the cliff face with cable launchers in class. They had learned to use their body's weight and hone their balance, correct their timing. They had done it over and over again. Next week, they would do it without cable launchers under the supervision of a Jedi Master. It would be one of their Force exercises.

He knew he should not be thinking of climbing it freehand. But he was. Qui-Gon wanted to gobble up the challenges the Jedi teachers threw at the students. A week was too long to wait. It wasn't so very high, really. It was just a big rock. There were handholds and footholds, even if he couldn't see them. If he fell, he would fall into the lake.

If he were caught, he would be in trouble. Then again, he wouldn't get caught. It was dawn and the lake area was deserted.

He heard the rustle behind him and turned. It was a fellow student, Tahl. She was in his class, but he didn't know her very well. She was slight, smaller than the rest of them. She looked like a little boy, he thought. He did not think of himself as a little boy.

She nodded at the cliff. "You thinking of climbing it?"

Startled, he was about to say no. But Jedi did not lie, even for small things. "Accustomed to the lie, you become," Yoda had warned them. "Easy it becomes to be false in big things, if false you are in small ones." So he said nothing.

To his surprise, she grinned. "Come on."

When he hesitated, she added, "Bet I can beat you to the top."

She ran and launched herself at the rock face, grabbing her first handhold. He hesitated for just a moment, surprised at how eagerly she attacked the rock. Then she seemed to mold herself against it. She waited until Qui-Gon ran forward and joined her.

It was harder than he'd thought. The handholds that seemed so firm to him with a cable on his belt now seemed impossibly tiny. The rock had become his enemy. It was tricky to keep his balance. Sweat began to pour down his face. His muscles shook with effort. He forgot about Tahl's challenge and concentrated on not falling off.

He was three-quarters of the way to the top when he looked over at her. They were neck and neck. Her face was grimy and sweaty. She grinned.

The grin spurred him on. He found the next handhold, then the next. She was behind him now, and he was almost there. He searched for the next handhold, his face pressed against the rough rock.

Suddenly she was beside him, climbing easily. Then she was ahead of him, her hand reaching for the top. She swung herself up and over, then sat, breathing hard.

Qui-Gon followed, feeling furious and ashamed. She had beaten him. When he turned to Tahl, he expected to see triumph in her eyes. Instead, he saw excitement.

"I felt it, Qui-Gon! I felt the Force!" She

slapped the ground, her green-gold eyes blazing. "The rock — it was part of me. I was part of . . . everything. Even the air! It was just the way Yoda said it would be."

Now he was envious as well as embarrassed.

"I can tell you what you did wrong," she said, nudging him with a shoulder. "You hated the rock. You fought it. I did, too, in the beginning. You need to love the rock."

Love the rock? That sounded silly. Qui-Gon wanted to tell her that. But he knew what she meant. And suddenly, he didn't want to hurt her feelings.

Tahl stood. "Now for the reward. Come on!" She ran forward and leaped off the end of the rock, straight into the shimmering green water.

Qui-Gon followed. It was a long drop, but the shock of the water felt refreshing. Tahl waited underwater for him. She grinned, and Qui-Gon smiled back. The cool water felt so good, and he had climbed the rock. Next time he would do better. Next time, he would love the rock.

They burst up to the surface. Tahl's dark hair was slicked back off her forehead. Now she looked like a water creature, sleek and supple.

Suddenly, she frowned. "Someone's coming," she murmured. "Do you see? Down by the path."

Qui-Gon said nothing. But a fraction of a second later, he noticed a disturbance in the overhanging leaves, far down the path.

"We're supposed to be in meditation right now," she whispered.

"This way," he said. He stroked to the edge of the lake, where a rocky outcropping would shield them.

They waited in the shadows, shivering a little from the coolness of the water. They heard the unmistakable sound of Yoda's shuffling step. Of all the Jedi Masters, for Yoda to catch them!

Qui-Gon's eyes narrowed in concern, but Tahl looked as though she would burst out laughing. Qui-Gon placed a hand over her mouth, and, grinning, she did the same to him.

Yoda stopped on the path over their heads. They did not breathe. After a moment, he moved on.

After Yoda had moved away, Tahl dropped her hand, and Qui-Gon dropped his.

"You know, you almost beat me to the top," she said. "We could be rivals. But I think it would be better if we were friends."

"Let's be friends," Qui-Gon agreed. He spoke soberly. He took friendship seriously. Already he knew he wanted to be friends with this girl.

As if she couldn't contain herself any longer, Tahl dived underwater and moved away from him. She came up, shaking off water. The sun was shining, and the rays made the droplets shimmer.

"Friends forever!" she called to him, treading water. "Deal?"

"Deal," he said.

Forever.

Qui-Gon was still waiting when Obi-Wan burst into the small waiting area in the med complex a few hours later.

"Any news?"

Qui-Gon shook his head. "They are still with her."

"Have you seen her?"

"Not since I got here. Soon, they say."

Eritha hurried in. "How is Tahl?"

"She is holding her own," Qui-Gon said. "Other than that, I don't know."

Eritha paced in front of him. "I don't understand why Manex had you bring her here. Well, I do. He always thinks what he has is the best. Where is he?"

"He waited with me for some time," Qui-Gon said. "He left to attend to some things at his home. He said he would be back."

She sat down and pressed her palms together. "I hate waiting. I know the Jedi don't feel that way."

"We hate it, too," Obi-Wan said. "We are just better at it."

Not so, Qui-Gon thought. The past two hours had been the hardest of his life.

Eritha waited for some minutes, then restlessly got up. "I need some air. Will you contact me as soon as we know something?"

Obi-Wan assured her that they would. He remained next to Qui-Gon, not speaking. Qui-Gon felt his Padawan's sympathy and concern. He was grateful for his presence. It was easier not to wait alone. He knew that Obi-Wan loved Tahl, too.

"Did Tahl say anything about the kidnapping?" Obi-Wan asked him quietly.

"Balog was looking for the list of informers, just as Irini and Lenz thought," Qui-Gon said. He briefly told Obi-Wan what Tahl had told him. He had trouble concentrating on the whys of Tahl's kidnapping. There would be time for that, as soon as he looked into her face and saw that she was her old self again.

"The message runner could be the key," Obi-

Wan mused. "We know the list was stolen and could have been in Absolute hands. What if Oleg took it? If Tahl was spotted escaping with him, they would of course suspect that she had it. Tahl said that the Absolute leaders wanted to interrogate Oleg. If they couldn't find him, they would turn to Tahl."

Qui-Gon was barely listening. "It is a theory, Padawan. We shall see."

The doors slid open, and the med team emerged. Qui-Gon and Obi-Wan stood. The doctor went straight to Qui-Gon.

"Her vital signs are dropping. We did everything we could do. The damage to her internal organs was severe. She will see you now."

Qui-Gon searched the doctor's face. "So she will recover."

"Her damage is severe," the doctor repeated. His weary eyes were full of sadness as he looked at Qui-Gon.

"She will recover," Qui-Gon repeated. This time there was certainty in his voice.

He strode past the doctor and hurried to the room where Tahl was kept. She lay in a diagnostic bed. He ignored the readouts and sensors. He took her hand, and she turned her head slowly toward him. He was relieved to see that the med team had removed the disguising lenses from her eyes. He had missed seeing Tahl's lovely green and gold eyes. Now the face he loved was before him, just as he had always known it. He knew every line and curve, every strong feature, every soft hollow.

He took her hand, but received no answering pressure. Qui-Gon ran his fingers down her bare arm to feel her skin. It was cold. So cold . . .

Her lips parted. He had to bend his head to hear her. "Wherever I am headed, I will wait for you, Qui-Gon. I've always been a solitary traveler."

"Not anymore," he said. "Remember? We will go on together. You promised," he teased. "You can't back out now. I'll never let you forget it."

Her smile and the slight pressure of her fingers seemed to cost her a great effort. Panic shot through him.

He brought his face close. He placed his forehead against hers. Her skin was so cool against his. He willed his own warmth and energy into her body. Of what benefit was his great strength, what was it good for, if it could not heal her? Qui-Gon called on everything he knew, everything he believed in — his connection to the Force, his great love for Tahl — to enter her and give her strength.

He felt a small sigh flutter against his cheek. Her fingers pressed his again. He knew that she had felt what he had tried to give her, and had received comfort from it. He had never felt so attuned to her, so close. If he could breathe for her, he would.

"Let my last moment be this one," she said.

He felt her breath go in, then out, soft against his cheek. Then it did not resume.

CHAPTER 20

Obi-Wan sat, his head in his hands. Suddenly, he straightened. He felt a disturbance in the Force. Something had been sucked out of the air, a powerful energy collapsing, leaving a vacuum.

When he heard the cry from the other room, at first he did not know who could have made it.

Then he realized it had been his Master.

He heard running feet in the corridor outside the waiting room. The med team.

He dashed to the door and activated it, then followed the med team into Tahl's room.

Two of the team checked the monitoring equipment. The doctor stood by. He did nothing.

That was when Obi-Wan fully understood that Tahl was gone.

The med team stood back from the equipment. No one tried to move the large man bent over the body in the bed. His grief was too huge, too private.

Tahl's eyes were closed. Her hand rested in Qui-Gon's. A slight smile was still on her face. His forehead was pressed against hers. He did not move a muscle. He did not let go of her hand.

Obi-Wan was staggered by the pain he felt in that room. The very lines of Qui-Gon's body told him of an agony so immense he could not grasp it. The intimacy of Qui-Gon's posture, the way his forehead rested against Tahl's, suddenly told Obi-Wan that he had not begun to realize the depths of Qui-Gon's feelings.

With that knowledge, his heart broke for his Master.

He took a step closer. How could he help Qui-Gon? What could he do?

Qui-Gon turned. Obi-Wan saw a face that had changed. Something was gone or something was added, he did not know. But it was no longer the face he knew so well. Grief had marked it forever. Obi-Wan knew that in his bones.

He would have his own grief for Tahl. It would never match Qui-Gon's.

He approached the bed slowly. He had no

words for this. Nothing he had learned at the Temple, nothing Qui-Gon had taught him, had prepared him for it.

He placed his hand on Qui-Gon's shoulder. "Let me help you, Master."

Qui-Gon's eyes were dead. "There is no help for me now."

Qui-Gon looked down at Tahl's lifeless body. His hand still clasped hers. "There is only revenge."

Visit
www.scholastic.com/starwars
and discover

The Early Adventures of
Obi-Wan Kenobi and Qui-Gon Jinn

JEDI APPRENTICE

☐ BDN 0-590-51922-0	#1: The Rising Force	$4.99 US
☐ BDN 0-590-51925-5	#2: The Dark Rival	$4.99 US
☐ BDN 0-590-51933-6	#3: The Hidden Past	$4.99 US
☐ BDN 0-590-51934-4	#4: The Mark of the Crown	$4.99 US
☐ BDN 0-590-51956-5	#5: The Defenders of the Dead	$4.99 US
☐ BDN 0-590-51969-7	#6: The Uncertain Path	$4.99 US
☐ BDN 0-590-51970-0	#7: The Captive Temple	$4.99 US
☐ BDN 0-590-52079-2	#8: The Day of Reckoning	$4.99 US
☐ BDN 0-590-52080-6	#9: The Fight for Truth	$4.99 US
☐ BDN 0-590-52084-9	#10: The Shattered Peace	$4.99 US
☐ BDN 0-439-13930-9	#11: The Deadly Hunter	$4.99 US
☐ BDN 0-439-13931-7	#12: The Evil Experiment	$4.99 US
☐ BDN 0-439-13932-5	#13: The Dangerous Rescue	$4.99 US
☐ BDN 0-439-13933-3	#14: The Ties That Bind	$4.99 US

Also available:

☐ BDN 0-590-52093-8	*Star Wars Journal:* Episode I: Anakin Skywalker	$5.99 US
☐ BDN 0-590-52101-2	*Star Wars Journal:* Episode I: Queen Amidala	$5.99 US
☐ BDN 0-439-13941-4	*Star Wars Journal:* Episode I: Darth Maul	$5.99 US
☐ BDN 0-590-01089-1	*Star Wars: Episode I—* The Phantom Menace	$5.99 US

Scholastic Inc., P.O. Box 7502, Jefferson City, MO 65102

Please send me the books I have checked above. I am enclosing $_____ (please add $2.00 to cover shipping and handling). Send check or money order–no cash or C.O.D.s please.

Name_____ Birthdate_____

Address_____

City_____ State/Zip_____

Please allow four to six weeks for delivery. Offer good in U.S.A. only. Sorry, mail orders are not available to residents of Canada. Prices subject to change.

SWA801

FIRST CAME *STAR WARS: EPISODE I*
COMING SOON IS *STAR WARS: EPISODE II*
IN BETWEEN THERE IS...

STAR WARS®
JEDI QUEST

After a death-defying pilgrimage to a sacred Jedi site, twelve-year-old Anakin Skywalker is sent with his Jedi master, Obi-Wan Kenobi, on a mission to defeat an evil foe. There, Anakin's gifts are tested—and Anakin is tempted by the darker fate that awaits him.

Wherever Books Are Sold

LUCAS BOOKS

■ SCHOLASTIC

SJQT1001